THE SHADOW OF DESIRE

THE
SHADOW
OF DESIRE

REBECCA STOWE

W.W. Norton & Company
New York • London

Book design by Debbie Glasserman

Stowe, Rebecca.
    The shadow of desire / Rebecca Stowe.
       p.   cm.
    ISBN 0-679-42066-5
    1. Divorced women—New York (N.Y.)—Psychology—Fiction.
    2. Family—Michigan—Fiction.   I. Title.
    PS3569.T6753S53   1996
    813'.54—dc20   95-39436

ISBN 0-393-31658-0

W. W. Norton & Company, Inc., 500 Fifth Avenue, New York, N.Y. 10110
W. W. Norton & Company Ltd., 10 Coptic Street, London WC1A 1PU

    2 3 4 5 6 7 8 9 0

This book is dedicated to my father,
Joseph G. Stowe,
and to the memory of my mother,
Elizabeth Robertson Stowe.

Those who restrain desire, do so because theirs is weak enough to be restrained; and the restrainer or Reason usurps its place & governs the unwilling.

And being restrain'd, it by degrees becomes passive, till it is only the shadow of desire.

—William Blake,
The Marriage of Heaven and Hell

THE SHADOW OF DESIRE

1952. IKE IS ELECTED; ROCKY MARCIANO BECOMES THE champ; polio invades; Lillian Hellman cannot cut her conscience to fit the year's fashions and Richard Nixon's dog is the most popular creature in the country. The H-bomb is exploded and I am born, the very next day, a mutant of sorts. I have all my fingers and toes, all the necessary parts in all the right places, all except one. I am born without a heart.

Or so Virginia says. Virginia is my mother; I am her namesake, Virginia Junior, Ginger for short. I call her Virginia rather than Mother because in 1960, when I was eight, she decided to liberate herself from the yoke of motherhood and become a Person. This was a great catastrophe for me, not because I resented her being a person—the truth being she would never be a "person" to me, she would always be a force, and that force was Mother—but because she insisted we all call her by her name. Not Mom, not dear, not honey, not Muu-ther, but Virginia. If we fell and came running into the house with a bloody skinned knee, crying for Mom, she'd turn her back and refuse to hand over the iodine and Band-Aids until we called her "Virginia." If Poppy came home and called, "Honey, what's for dinner?" he didn't get any.

It was humiliating. "You call your mother by her *name?*" my little friends would ask, in amazement and fear, as if calling my mother "Virginia" would explode the very structure of all our lives, for what was more safe and secure than "Mom"? What if this becoming-a-person thing was catching and they'd lose their own mothers, whose names most of them didn't even know? Everyone felt sorry for me and avoided my house when Virginia was there. They couldn't stand the embarrassment of having to call her "Virginia" rather than Mrs. Moore, which was who she was and always would be to them, it was like asking them to turn their backs on all their training, all the rules, and that was asking too much.

The person my mother became was not the one she wanted to be, although I don't think she had anything specific in mind. She just wanted to be "her own woman," and if she wasn't quite sure who that was, it didn't matter, she knew who she wasn't: Mom-Mother-honey-dear. She was not a stupid woman, far from it. She was smart, perhaps even brilliant. She had graduated with highest honors from the University of Georgia, one of the few women in her class. She was one of the few local mothers with a college degree, and looking back on it, I wonder how she could have been so simpleminded, how she could have thought that forcing a bunch of terrified children to call her by her first name would somehow result in her attaining a sense of self. All it did was turn her into an eccentric heretic in the eyes of others, and eventually she found that unbearable. She had neither the strength nor the fury to defy the consensus, and unfortunately for us all, but especially for her, her experiment in Personhood was a disaster.

2

FOR MOST OF MY LIFE I HAVE BEEN FLEEING. THE DIRECTION always seems to be away from Virginia, that is always my intention, but no matter which way I run she is always there, standing in front of me, real or imagined, like some kind of spectre of doom.

"Why do you go?" Cassie always asks, and I never know what to tell her. I don't know why I make this annual Christmas pilgrimage to Michigan with a trunkful of dirty laundry. There's something almost shameful about the laundry, something so teenagerish about driving all the way through New York State and across a strip of Ontario, 650 miles one way, with no clean clothes. So undignified. So unlike the way I think I should be, at my age, at this stage in my life.

And what is it I think I should be? I don't know; I'm not any more clear on that than Virginia was, but instead of thinking I should be More, I think I should be Farther. Farther along with my career, farther away from North Bay, farther from my past, farther along in my own quest for Personhood.

If it weren't for the snow I would love this drive. I love being alone in the car, I feel self-contained and in control, if only for twelve hours. I love the idea of being unreachable—no phones, no newspapers, no television, free to inhabit any world I choose, free to let my mind wander uninhibited by the chaos of the real world, which terrifies me. Not in any physical sense; I'm not afraid of muggers lurking in dark doorways or murderers rustling about in the bushes in Central Park or angry gangs of girls running up and down the sidewalks with hat pins to jab into unsuspecting shoppers, even though these threats are real enough. It is, ironically, their very realness that makes me not fear them: because they are real, one can take precautions, one avoids dark doorways and stays out of Central Park after the sun sets and crosses to the other side of the street when fifty kids start running toward you. In fact, I'm rather fearless, physically. It's the one bit of my youthfulness I retain, that sense of immortality, that thoughtless, baseless sense that nothing could ever happen to *me*.

No, what I am afraid of is more amorphous, less substantial. I don't know how to describe it without sounding like a crank, someone who should be wandering around Times Square in a sandwich board reading BEWARE THE INVADERS! or some such nonsense. What I fear is the way I feel every time I venture out of my apartment. I feel bombarded by the world, attacked by all the information, all the messages, all the subtle and blatant injunctions to do this, be that, wear this, buy that, all of which are designed to make one feel inadequate. And which succeed, in my case. I simply can't block them out, as everyone else seems to be able to do. I sometimes think that I missed the evolutionary boat, that somewhere along the line our species developed a gene for blocking out the unnecessary, for creating a little sievelike device in our brains to strain out the superfluous, and I didn't get it.

"Maybe that's why I never had children," I told Cassie. "I instinctively knew it was my duty to the species to remove myself from the gene pool," but she thinks that's unlikely. "I think it has more to do with your fear of the living than your concern for the unborn," she always says and she's probably right.

I check the odometer. Four hundred miles to go. I always promise myself to stop along the way, to see Niagara Falls again or go to the Women's Rights National Park. "What is that?" I always ask myself as I pass the sign, what kind of feminist am I, passing it by twice a year, on my way to and from North Bay, why don't I stop? But I am always in a hurry. A hurry to get it over with when I am on my way there, a hurry to get home when I'm on my way back to New York.

"What are you in such a hurry about?" Virginia always asks, and I'm not quite sure. Nothing in my life is particularly urgent. With the exception of my classes, I have no solid commitments. All my obligations are rather vague, open-ended, but, for the most part, that's how I like it. I love doing what I do, but it's time-consuming, all-encompassing, it takes years to discover enough about a life to write it.

That's why I prefer the dead to the living. As subjects, that is. The dead aren't going anywhere. There is nothing to keep up with, no fear that the knowledge you obtain will be obsolete by the time you understand what it *means*.

The dead are at one and the same time both more mysterious and more accessible than the living, for no matter how complex they were—no matter how complicated their lives or how ambivalent their feelings, their thoughts, their deeds—they remain the same. The dead can be puzzling, but one can always find the pieces and put them together, whereas the living are not complete. There are always missing pieces, and generally the missing pieces are the most important ones, the key images without which the portrait is indecipherable.

The truth is, one is never complete until one is dead. And one is never understandable, to others, until one is six feet under, the longer the better, at least in terms of accumulating information. Although not *too* long, of course; too long dead can pose as many problems as not dead, as any biographer of Shakespeare can attest. With the too long dead one must make a lot from a little; with the not dead, one must make a little from a lot.

I prefer the obscure dead. "That's for sure," Virginia often says. "Where do you come up with these women?" She thinks I should write about someone more contemporary. Herself, for instance. "It would make a wonderful book," she says, "everything's there. The southern gothic childhood. The crazy aunts and the Confederate ghosts, my famous mother, my beaux . . ." She trails off, wandering back to Georgia, back to a childhood half remembered and half fantasy, drifting back into her drawl as she conjures up images of leading cotillions and sipping mint juleps under two-hundred-year-old oak trees dripping with Spanish moss, images familiar to me from *Gone with the Wind,* which is where she no doubt got them.

I love my work. Being a biographer is like being a detective, a psychiatrist, an anthropologist, and a social historian all in one. One has a tremendous amount of power, it is truly like bringing the dead back to life, like being Frankenstein without the moral dilemma: if one's subject turns out to be a monster (as a number of mine have), one at least has the consolation of knowing it's not a monster of one's own creation.

Every discovery is a treasure, even the ones that blow your theories to smithereens. A theory is, after all, just a theory, up for grabs, something to be proved or disproved, whereas what has already been lived cannot be changed.

I had to come to terms with that when I was working on my first book, *The Obscure Muse*, a biography of Angeline Wilton. Angeline's father and brother, Sir Henry and Frederick, were both hugely successful eighteenth-century novelists, although they, too, are forgotten now except by a few academicians. They churned out immensely popular romances, the most famous of which are *The Fountain of Landymere* and *The Misfortunes of Master Manfred*. They kept Angeline a virtual prisoner at the family estate in Essex, where in addition to doing all their secretarial work and acting as hostess, she wrote several volumes of poetry, one of which survives to this day. "So fair, so far, so true . . . ," that's Angeline. In any case, my theory was that Angeline was the far superior writer of the three and that if she hadn't been forced into slavery in the service of their careers, she could have made a lasting contribution to literature.

I was young; it was the 1970s, I was hot on the trail of all of "Shakespeare's sisters," as Virginia Woolf called them, all the women of talent and imagination who had been lost to posterity because of their sex. I had come across numerous references to a novel Angeline had written—published anonymously—and I was determined to find it and resurrect both Angeline and her work, to carry her out of the grave and put her back in the world where she belonged.

It was a rather monumental task: I had neither title nor author, just a vague plot outline I had culled from her journals. I was living in London at the time, in a brutally cold bed-sit in Maida Vale, surviving on Digestives and Silk Cuts and dreams, bathing as infrequently as hygiene would allow, stalking my quarry on foot to save my 10p coins for the ravenous gas fire. I kept myself going on fantasies, imagining myself at the MLA convention, telling a lecture hall full of admiring colleagues about my fortuitous discovery, being approached by Lionel Trilling about an opening at Columbia, moving to New York, living in a huge apartment overlooking the Hudson, a huge subsidized apartment with central heat and a bathroom where I could take long, hot baths without feeding coins into the hot-water meter. I might even find a lover. It had been a long time since I'd touched anything living, besides my sickly geranium. A lover would be nice, someone brilliant, a medievalist, perhaps, medievalists were incredibly sexy and passionate. I had no idea why this was so, but it had been my experience that all medievalists were remarkably attractive, not necessarily physically, but they all had an aliveness, a kind of charged, urgent enthusiasm I found irresistible. It made no sense to me—personally, I couldn't imagine getting worked up about *Beowulf*, but then again, I'm sure there are tens of millions of people who can't imagine why I get so worked up about my dead women.

I finally tracked down an ancient woman named Amelia Fortunata, who had an attic filled with boxes and boxes of old books, manuscripts, newspapers, magazines. She collected absolutely everything she came across that had anything to do with London literary life in the eighteenth century, "Just in case someone needs it." She was a delightful old kook, gray-haired, chirpy, and absentminded, dressed in nubby old tweeds and looking like she just stepped out of the 1950s. She'd bring up a pot of tea and sit on an old trunk and jabber away about Kitty Clive and Dr. Johnson, as if they were old pals. Amelia Fortunata was not a librarian: nothing was organized, it was all just there, the worthless jumbled in with the priceless, a dusty mess, and I would make the long trek from Maida Vale to Shepherd's Bush, filled with hope on the way there and discouragement on the way back.

To make a long story boring, as my father always says, I finally found it, in manuscript. I recognized Angeline's tiny, obsessive, chicken-scratch penmanship immediately. *The Abduction of Abigail.* I was overjoyed: I grabbed Mrs. Fortunata and danced around the attic with her, for she, too, was ecstatic—this was why she collected all this, "Just in case." She wrapped it up for me in newspaper, like a fish-and-chips dinner, and I ran back to my bed-sit with my treasure tucked under my arm, thinking that my fortune was made.

It wasn't. The novel wasn't terrible, but it wasn't very good, either. Needless to say, I was rather depressed. Too depressed to see what I really had in my hands. Too depressed by all the flashing eyes and saintly dead mothers and bloated blue bodies floating in murky Scottish lochs to see that what I had was not just another overwrought romance but evidence—no, proof!—that Angeline had not been her father's and brother's amanuensis but rather had been the real author of their books.

The Obscure Muse set me on my way. I was beginning with Angeline but I had plans, dreams, I would rescue from obscurity hundreds of brilliant women, thousands of them.

I was obsessed with a very specific type of woman, one who seemed to suffer from a certain type of paralysis. Women who had all the equipment—the brains, the skill, the talent, the desire, the ambition, the leisure, and the money— to accomplish as much if not more than the men in their lives but who could not, for some reason, *do.* Why were there so many of them? Feminism has, of course, given us many answers, but I was searching for something very specific: I was interested in women who not only couldn't do, but who were tormented by it. Women who would reach a certain point and then stop, as if grabbed from beyond by an invisible rope that held them there, struggling, miserable, baffled—Dostoyevsky's screamers and Freud's hysterics, paralyzed, but not quiet.

"In that case, why don't you write a book about me?" Virginia always asks. She's one of three women who want me to write their lives: the other two are Melanie Fraser, a friend of mine from high school, and Mrs. Cortez, my next-door neighbor and biggest fan, although I doubt she's ever made it all the way through any of my books. But she likes having them; she buys them and comes to my readings; she likes being a fan of someone she can borrow a cup of sugar from, which gives her a leg up on her friends, who are only fans of people they don't know.

They are all three alcoholics. Do they drink because they can't do, or can they not do because they drink? Who knows? It's easy to blame the booze, as easy as blaming society or education or male domination, all of which are very real problems, but none of them holds the answer I'm searching for. As for demon rum, as far as I'm concerned, alcoholism has nothing to do with my quest, for the truth of the matter is, there have been a great many women who drank and were still able to do, a greater number who don't drink at all but still can't move a muscle.

Mrs. Cortez is very discreet about her desire, she only hints. Perhaps she could pay *someone* to write a book about her; she's seen a lot in her day. No doubt she has, I tell her, why doesn't she try to write it herself? Oh no, she would never be able to do that, but *someone else* could do it.

Melanie calls me about twice a year, either on her way to or from a rehab, to blame me, if she's drunk, or to apologize, if she's not. It's my fault she's a drunk because we started drinking together when we were fifteen; I owe it to her, therefore, to write a book about her. "I only write about dead people," I always tell her and she says no problem, she's going to kill herself as soon as she hangs up.

Her threats don't worry me, they just make me sad. She thinks that if I wrote her life, it would have been justified, and as much as I would like to give her that, I can't. She wants to give me her life, to stuff it in a cardboard box and ship it UPS to my office with a little note: "Here, *you* make something of it," and I suppose if I were a novelist I could, I could take Melanie's tragic little life and make something beautiful and moving and possibly even grand out of it, but that is entirely beyond my scope. I am not terribly imaginative. I've known it all my life, ever since I was a child and I would lie on the beach with my little friends, looking up at the sky, and they would see animals and sailing ships and cartoon characters while I saw just plain clouds. This lack of imagination is a great disappointment to me, but I know that we must play out our lives with the cards we've been dealt and the hand I got was plodding and methodical rather than visionary.

"Boring," Michael calls my hand. "Boring, boring, bor-ring."

Michael is my sometimes lover, he bounces in and out of my life on some sort of bizarre insect-like schedule that only he understands. I'm not quite sure what it is we have to-gether—if I so much as whisper the word "relationship" he breaks out in hives and runs away, so I call it our "whatever-it-is." He is the grasshopper to my ant—Michael lives in the now, now, now. In fact he makes his living by the "now." He's what they call Hot, bright-red-burning-hot, late-night-television-hot, T-shirt-advertisement-hot. He is currently glaring out from every third bus-stop shelter in Manhattan: angry, defiant, satiric, and incredibly pleased with himself in his pocket T with the sleeves rolled up rebelliously over what

I can assure you is a fake tattoo. Michael, for all his tough-guy posturing, is an absolute coward when it comes to pain. He's also pathologically terrified of AIDS, something one would never guess from the amount of sleeping around he does.

"Then why are you with me?" I always ask, when he insinuates the hand I got dealt was not a "keeper." It's a good question and he always disappears for a while, a week, a month, half a year, to ponder it. He comes back, answerless, and we begin again, lovers until the next time he wakes up and wonders what the fuck he's doing with a dinosaur.

I sometimes think that Michael keeps coming back because he too wants me to be his biographer, a Boswell he can sleep with if the urge strikes, but I have no intention of writing a life in which I am a part, and not a very significant one at that. The brighter he grows, the more insignificant I become, until what was once a chapter is now merely a footnote. Ginger Moore—asterisk.

I sometimes feel like a mere footnote in Virginia's life as well, but that's not why I won't write it. I'm not blind; I know that my obsession with paralyzed women is about her, and about myself as well, for I'm not fully convinced in my heart that writing about women who can't do qualifies as doing. It certainly did for Betty Friedan and Simone de Beauvoir, but they were pioneers and I am merely a Ginger-come-lately, trying to find answers beyond the obvious ones.

I should take a moment to introduce the Panel of Judges, my lifetime companions, my internal party-poopers, my tireless and ever-vigilant critics. I have metamorphosed them into a revolving group of celebrity panelists who dwell in my mind solely to remind me of what a worthless excuse for a human being I am. Right now, the Panel consists of George Bernard Shaw, Jonathan Edwards, H. L. Mencken and, in an occasional guest appearance, Virginia. I have a knack for dredging up from the dead, and, less frequently, from the living, the perfect critics for the occasion, ones who will brilliantly and articulately grind me into mush.

They had a ball with *The Obscure Muse,* my book about Angeline. "You call this scholarship?" they shrieked. "Where's the ideas?" "Who cares about this twit?" "A monkey with a computer could write better than this." "Yawn." And so forth.

The first sign for the bridge to the U.S. appears. In another half-hour I'll be home, or rather, at my parents' house. North Bay is no longer "home," but I can't quite bring myself to think of my ratty little tenement apartment as "home," either, even though I've lived there ten years, even though I love New York, even though all my friends are there, my work is there, my sometimes lover is there, my life is there. It still somehow doesn't feel *real,* in fact it sometimes feels as if I'm play-acting at living. No, not even that, it's more as if I'm *watching* my own life, waiting in the wings, watching this half-formed creature who is myself until the time is right for me to make my entrance.

I sometimes fear I've waited too long. It's beginning, the creeping transparency of middle age. It hasn't fully engulfed me yet but the process has begun: a wrinkle here, a sag there and within no time at all I will be enveloped in that grayness that renders women invisible. I've been expecting it—being born at the tail end of the Baby Boom has its advantages and disadvantages. One knows what's coming but by the time it arrives it has been explored, discussed, serialized, TV-movied and talk-showed to death, to the point where it hardly counts as an experience of one's own. It seems somehow fraudulent, barren, meaningless. Even though I am a Baby Boomer myself, I can fully understand why young people today despise us—it's as if we have claimed every experience, every feeling, every idea for ourselves, as if there were neither a past nor a future.

As always, I tense up as I approach the customs booths on the American side of the bridge: three of my former high school teachers moonlight at Immigration, and although I'm always happy to see Mr. O'Toole, my Civics teacher, or Miss Ulrich, my American Lit teacher, I always fear I'll pull up to the booth and see Mr. Hegley, who has remained with me all these years as an occasional Guest Judge on the Panel. Mr. Hegley, who told me back in tenth grade that I wasn't college material, that I should just stay home and "make babies" because that was all I was cut out for. He tends to pop up whenever I'm stuck with a project, when I'm at that point when I've gathered together all my research and I've got it all spread out before me on the living room floor, a huge jumble of notes, books, articles, letters, journals, and I'm overwhelmed by the massiveness of the task before me. I begin to feel like Psyche, stuck in a room with a pile of grain to sort, and I think I'll never be able to do it. I know the gods won't send an army of ants to help me out and I begin to hear Mr. Hegley's voice, taunting and snide, telling me I should have listened to him, he told me I wasn't smart enough to do anything with my life, I could have at least had a family, but no, I wouldn't listen, and now I have nothing, and so on. There is no arguing with the Judges. I can't say, "But wait, what about my books, don't they count?" for the answer is "No." Nothing counts. I cannot possibly please them. If I gave up tomorrow, if I somehow corralled Michael into marrying me and got pregnant and had as many children as I could before the onset of menopause, that wouldn't count either because even though it might shut up Mr. Hegley, he'd just disappear from the Panel, to be replaced by Benjamin Spock, who would berate my mothering.

I pull up to the booth slowly, full of dread, but it's someone I've never seen before, a young man who doesn't even look at me as he asks me where I was born, where I live now, where I'm going. He doesn't care, it's just his job. He waves me through without a word, as if dismissing a servant, and as I drive down the ramp I think about when I was young, when Melanie and Maggie Pittsfield and Cindy Tucker and I would load up my Volkswagen bug and drive over to Grand Bend or Ipperwash and we'd stop at the customs booth and flirt with the inspectors and Melanie would have them in tears laughing as she jabbered away in her made-up language: "Onamonapea alla cokeala roun da corner," she'd say, and we became the Cokeala Roun Da Corner Girls to all the inspectors, gabbing and flirting while the traffic piled up behind us.

"How can you be so selfish?" Virginia screamed at me once, when she had been in one of the cars stuck behind us. "You think you're so cute, you think you're so charming, but just you wait, one of these days you won't be so cute anymore and you won't like it one little bit when you're the one doing the waiting."

I turn down Raddison Boulevard, circling around the house so I can see into the kitchen before I pull into the driveway. Virginia is sitting alone at the kitchen table, waiting for dinner, waiting for me, and I want to keep right on going, to circle around the house and back to Iroquois Avenue, back to the bridge, back home, but I force myself to turn the car into the driveway. Virginia jumps up as the headlights flash on the refrigerator, and any second now she'll be standing in the doorway, with the light from the kitchen shining behind her, illuminating her desperation, her need, but only for a second. She'll shake it off, laugh, shout "Well, look what the cat dragged in!" and Poppy and Cease will appear behind her and the annual Passion Play will begin.

3

"'HE WHO DESIRES BUT ACTS NOT BREEDS PESTILENCE.' Blake. *Proverbs of Hell*."

Virginia smiles triumphantly after her recitation and the rest of us, Poppy, Cecil Junior, and myself, squirm uncomfortably in our chairs as she plops the dinner dishes on the table.

"You should use that as your epigraph," she tells me, and Cease, the comedian of the family, says, "No, *you* should use it as your epitaph."

"Oh, no," Virginia says, not in the least dismayed, "I already have my epitaph. 'She came, she saw, she crumbled.'" She turns to me. "Write it down," she says.

As if I needed to. She's been telling us that for decades. She loves to talk about her death, as if it were imminent, but with the exception of hangovers, she hasn't been sick in years, and despite her drinking and smoking she will probably outlive us all.

"Well," Poppy says, tucking his napkin into his collar, "isn't this terrific? Just like old times."

"Yeah," Cease says, "except *Virginia's* still standing up."

"Cecil Augustus Moore, Junior!" Poppy says. "Don't start in on that."

"It's all right, Cecil," Virginia says, "it's true. Cease has never forgiven me for being a drunk, have you, dear?"

"Nope," he says, stuffing his mouth full of scalloped potatoes, "and I never will."

Virginia shrugs and takes a swig of her drink.

"Perhaps I'll pass out with my head in the salad. Would that make you happy?"

Cease grunts. "It would make it more like 'old times,'" he says.

"Cheer up," Virginia says, reaching across the table and patting Cease's stubbly cheek, "the night is young. I may do something embarrassing yet."

"Now, now, now," Poppy says, "let's not dwell on the past," as if Virginia's drunkenness was ancient history, a bad dream from which we had all awakened. It used to infuriate me, his denial as they called it at Alateen, where I spent most of my youth, in stuffy hot basements listening to everyone talk about how rotten their lives were instead of going on hayrides or whatever it was "normal" kids did, but now I am resigned. If thinking that Virginia's drunkenness is a thing of the past is comforting to him, let him have that. She's unlikely to change, and short of tying her up in a straitjacket and sending her shrieking off to a rehab, there isn't much he can do. It's his way of dealing with it, and after all, he is the one who has to live with her. Cease and I are just passing through, on our annual pilgrimage to pay our dutiful respects, fulfilling our moral obligation, so to speak. The commandment says to honor thy father and mother, but it doesn't say how often.

Poppy turns to me and grins. "So," he says, "how's Harvey?"

"Harvey" is what he calls Michael, what he's called all my invisible lovers. If I don't bring them home, they must not exist; or if they do undoubtedly exist, as Michael must, since Poppy saw him on the TV, they must not exist in *my* life, only in my imaginary life.

"He's fine," I say, as if I knew. "He's out in Hollywood, shooting a movie."

"What's he shooting it with, a howitzer?" Cease cries, nearly choking on his steak, and Poppy chuckles appreciatively. He wants to know if Jimmy Stewart is in the movie, and Cease thinks that's hilarious. "Is he playing a ten-foot-tall pink rabbit?" he asks and I tell him that would be cute but I believed he was playing himself.

"I suppose you don't bring him home because of me," Virginia says.

"Not at all," I say, "I don't bring him home because our schedules conflict." Not to mention our personalities. I leave that out, I would never tell either of my parents anything about my personal life, and even though we speak on the phone once a week, every Saturday when the rates go down, they know nothing about my life other than the fact that I live in New York, write books nobody reads, and teach at "some Jewish place." They never ask and I don't volunteer; it's as if my life apart from them has no relevance and therefore no interest.

"If you wanted to, you could make them not conflict," Virginia says. "It's because you're ashamed of me. You think I'll embarrass you."

She is determined to blame herself and so I let her, even though the truth of the matter is that I am protecting her from Michael rather than the other way around, protecting her and myself as well, from having him take her and turn her into some kind of pathetic parody of Amanda Wingfield: "Take my girlfriend's mother. Please. Ha ha. No, really, this woman is unbelievable, straight out of Tennessee Williams. 'Not one gentleman caller? It can't be true! There must be a flood, there must have been a tornado!'"

Poppy wants to change the subject. "What do you say we play Monopoly after dinner?" he suggests and we all groan.

"What?" he says. "I thought you *liked* Monopoly."

"*You* like Monopoly," Virginia says, "I loathe it."

Cease says that's because she always loses.

"I loathe losing," she says and Cease begins to giggle.

"I've got an idea," he says, and I can hear the gleeful, rumbling timbre in his voice, which means he's got a bomb and he's just waiting for the right time to drop it. "Let's *make* a board game."

"What kind of board game?" Poppy wants to know.

Cease grins. "Dysfunctional Families," he says. "The Game."

"Charming," Virginia says.

"No, wait," Cease says, "it's brilliant! All the questions have to do with famous dysfunctional families throughout history. It'll be educational as well as entertaining. Like, 'What New England woman gave her mother forty whacks?'"

"Lizzie Borden!" Poppy cries, as if we're already playing and now he's ahead.

"Yeah, you've got the idea," Cease says, glaring at Poppy.

"I object," Virginia says. "All your games are anti-mother."

Cease ignores her. "Or, 'Who killed his father and married his mother?'"

"Oedipus!" Poppy shouts, way out in front now, thoroughly pleased with himself and the new game.

"That's pronounced E-dipus," Virginia says, "not Ed-ipus." But nobody cares, we know who he meant.

"I've got one," I say. "How many relatives did Richard III

have to murder before getting the crown?" But Cease rolls his eyes and says that's too hard, they have to be questions *anybody* could answer.

"Like, 'What North Bay mother ruined her son's life by showing up as Class Mother wearing nothing but a mink coat?'"

I am astonished by how well she takes it, like an old pugilist expecting every movement to be a blow. She flinches, but she doesn't cry out.

Poppy is furious. "That's about enough from you, young man," he says but the moment the words are out of his mouth he realizes how ludicrous it is. Cease is forty-one years old, approaching middle age, hardly someone Poppy can send to his room without supper.

"It's all right, dear," Virginia says. "Look at the bright side. If Ginger won't immortalize me in a book, I can at least be an answer in a board game."

The subject is dropped and we finish our meal in silence. We are, after all, WASPs, noted not for our outbursts but rather for our ability to hold grudges into eternity, arriving at the Pearly Gates with a notebook filled with the names of people with whom we're not speaking.

After dinner, Cease takes off for Squeegee's to get drunk. He seems to think that making an ass out of himself and risking both his own life and that of anyone who has the misfortune to be on the same road with him is some kind of punishment to Virginia, but the fact of the matter is she's usually so drunk herself she can't tell the difference.

"You mean, you're named after your mother and your brother is named after your father?" Michael once asked. "Jeez, that's some narcissistic shit."

I'm sure they regret it now. Neither of us have turned out to be the paragons we were intended to be, though I'm not quite the embarrassment Cease is.

"Well, at least he doesn't live here," Virginia always says, and if he really wanted to punish her, that's exactly what he'd do, move back to North Bay, back home with them, and be the humiliation to her that she was to him.

It's not that he actually *does* anything, in fact it's just the opposite, he does virtually nothing.

"Like wash," Virginia says. "He didn't get that from me. No matter how bad things got, I always kept the house clean."

Her memory isn't altogether precise—the part about the house being clean is right, but it was I who did it. I'm not complaining; I don't make myself out to be some poor little Cinderella mopping the hearth while Virginia lay passed out on the porch swing. Although that's usually where she was. I *liked* cleaning the house; I *liked* scrubbing and vacuuming and making everything shine, just like the women on the TV, on *Lady of Charm*. It gave me a sense of order, and a sense of purpose that I otherwise wouldn't have had, living in the chaos that was our home back then. And it's stood me in good stead ("Just what does that *mean*?" Michael always asks when I use that phrase. "What the fuck is a *stead*?") not in the sense that I'm a good housekeeper—I'm not, my apartment is a disaster area—but in the sense that it gave me the patience to do the more plodding, unexciting parts of my work: organizing thousands of pages of notes, categorizing, cross-referencing, sifting through mountains of tedious, useless material to find the one tiny nugget of gold.

Poppy has escaped to his study, where he's writing his memoirs, pecking out his life letter by letter. "He thinks he's Laurence Sterne," Virginia says. "He's on page four hundred something and he's only three years old. He'll die before he gets to me."

I would like to escape, too, to plead some important task and hide in my childhood bedroom until Virginia clumps up the stairs and passes out, but I can't. I can't just leave her here, alone, sitting at the kitchen table with her bottle and her crossword-puzzle book, waiting for seven-thirty so she can go in the den and watch *Wheel of Fortune.*

It drives me crazy, this obsession of hers for that stupid game show. "How can you watch that mindless crap?" I ask her and she gets all huffy. "I *like* it," she whines, "I know all the answers."

She calls me an intellectual snob and pouts. I have nothing against television. Well, actually, I think it's the single most destructive element in modern life, but other than that, I have nothing against it. It isn't television itself I object to— I'm sure there is, as Michael is constantly telling me, plenty of "good stuff" on TV—nor is it even the sillier programs, or the commercials. It's the isolation it encourages, the false sense of companionship and camaraderie. Of course it's easy to see why one might prefer a family of wise-cracking, good-natured oafs to whomever it is one has to live with in real life, but it gets rather dangerous when one begins to think of them as one's "friends."

Last year when I was here, Cease and I drove down to Detroit to go Christmas shopping and all the way he kept quoting "Norm": Norm this and Norm that, Norm said and Norm did, all with the assumption that I knew who "Norm" was. I kept digging through my memory, trying to come up with a Norm from high school, someone with whom Cease had been friendly, but Cease had not been very popular, in fact I didn't remember his having any friends at all.

"Who's Norm?" I finally asked and he looked over at me.

"Oh, Ginger, come *on,*" he said and I started digging afresh but I couldn't excavate any Norm from my memory, except Norm Bradley, who I thought had died in Vietnam.

"Norm Bradley?" I asked. "I thought he was dead."

"He *is* dead, you moron," Cease said. "I'm talking about *Norm*."

"Well, who's *Norm*?" I asked.

He was furious. "*Norm,*" he growled. "*Norm.* From *Cheers.*"

He didn't speak to me the rest of the drive back to North Bay. I wasn't sure what was more upsetting, Cease's "friendship" with a TV character or my own shame at not knowing who he was. It was as if my not watching *Cheers* was a personal insult to Cease, as if I were putting myself above him by not watching a television show.

"Look," I said, "I'm sorry. I'm sure it's a great show. It must be. Half the country watches it."

"Not half," Cease sneered. "*Everybody* watches *Cheers.* Everybody except snobs like you."

"How can I watch it?" I asked, "I don't own a TV," but that, of course, was the point—my not watching TV put a barrier between us, a concrete roadblock neither one of us was willing to crash through. Since Cease wouldn't speak to me I spent the rest of the drive thinking about television as yet another excuse for polarization, pitting the TV-watchers against the nonwatchers. It was the nonwatchers, the minority, who were seen as suspect, as if we were trying to destroy the happiness and well-being of millions simply by not tuning in, as if we were passing judgment, as if we made them feel guilty, but it's not that at all, at least not in my case. I simply prefer to read, books are my escape route of choice, and I don't see why Cease has to get mad at me for it.

Michael was right; I was a dinosaur. "The only thing you're on the cutting edge of is extinction," he once said, and I suppose that's true.

And now Virginia was mad at me because I'd insulted her "program." She'd use that as her nightly excuse for getting drunk, as if she needed one at this point. The only interesting thing about her excuses was how creative she could get in coming up with one—"Your father wore that disgusting tie his sister gave him and it gave me a headache so I had to have a drink," and so on.

"Why don't we get out the Christmas decorations?" I suggest. "We can surprise Poppy and Cease by having the house all decorated by tomorrow morning."

But no, she doesn't want to decorate the house. She doesn't feel very Christmassy.

"I am not in the giving vein today," she says. "In fact, I'm not in the giving vein *any* day." She picks up her drink and wobbles into the den.

"I'm going to watch my program, if no one objects," she says and plops down in her chair to play the only game she can "win."

4

"ALL BIOGRAPHERS UNDERSTANDABLY SEEK A MEASURE OF fame for themselves," Leon Edel says. It's true, of course, but I don't like to think about it. It makes me feel as though I were using my dead women in order to promote myself, to justify my own life rather than theirs.

"My girlfriend's a necrophiliac," Michael says in one of his routines. "She feeds off the dead." He goes into a kind of *Night of the Living Dead* parody, but instead of ghoulish corpses sucking on the bones of the living he has ghoulish me slobbering over the poor dead in their peaceful graves.

This is generally followed by the routine in which he pillories me for being a WASP. "You ever go out with a WASP?" he asks his audience. "Don't. My girlfriend's a WASP, this woman takes the Protestant work ethic to new heights. She always has to be *doing* something, WASPs are always *doing* something, they're always busy, busy, busy, they should be called BEES, not WASPs. Busy Ethnic Episcopalian Skinflints. You ever try to have phone sex with a WASP? 'Oh, baby, I'm getting hard,' I say. 'Oh,' she coos, 'that's nice.' *Nice?* Yeah, well, okay. 'Baby,' I moan, 'I can feel your wet mouth moving up my thigh . . .' *Rrrrrr,* I hear in the background, *rrrrrr.* 'What's that?' I ask, and it stops. 'Ooooooh,' she purrs, 'you were saying?' Yeah, where was I? Oh yeah, her hot mouth is moving up my thigh, she's rubbing her tits against my leg. *Rrrrrr. Rrrrrrr.* 'What are you *doing?*' I ask, and she says, 'Nothing, honey, ooooo.' *Rrrrr, rrrrrr,* and I realize she's running the garbage disposal while I'm trying to fuck her. She's supposed to be creaming her pants and instead she's chopping up the goddam leftovers. I don't need to tell you what that did to my boner . . ." and so on.

Let me assure you, I don't have phone sex with Michael or anyone else and it's not because I'm a WASP prude. Both Michael and I have portable phones; the chances of someone overhearing the conversation are just too great. One year, I got Poppy and Virginia a portable phone for Christmas, thinking it would make their lives easier—Poppy could go out in the backyard and pick berries while he got the latest stock quotations; Virginia would never have to hang up because she needed to go in the kitchen to refill her drink. They loved it, at first, until one night when Virginia was in the den, watching *Wheel of Fortune,* and she suddenly heard voices on the TV other than those of Vanna and Pat Sajak. "I thought perhaps I was getting the DTs," she told me, "but no, there it was, clear as a bell, a woman's voice, saying, 'What time?' and your father's voice saying, 'After ten, she's always asleep by ten.' He meant passed out. 'I miss you, Cecil,' the woman's voice said, and he had the nerve to tell her he missed her, too. I was beside myself. I marched right into his den, where he was supposed to be working on that stupid book of his, and there he was, yakking away to that woman he swore he got rid of. I grabbed the phone and said, 'She won't be passed out tonight, however,' and hung up."

The portable phone ended up at the Salvation Army, and Poppy, as far as I know, continued to see "that woman," but at least Virginia could pretend not to know. It wasn't the fact that he was sleeping with someone else that bothered Virginia—"Better her than me," she's said more than once—it was having it flaunted in her face, having to endure the clumsy, supposedly well-meaning "hints" from her friends, the glum, hangdog faces full of pity staring at her whenever the subject of infidelity came up, and then, having to listen to "that woman's" feathery voice interrupting Virginia's "program," that was just too much.

"She'll probably get more pages in his book than I will," she always says. "He hates dwelling on the negative. That's me. The great negative of his life."

Click. Click. Click. Poppy's life is unfolding in his office, what used to be Cease's and my playroom. I don't remember ever having a very good time in there. I hope Poppy is having more fun than we did.

"Tristram," Virginia calls him when he's working, and I wonder what he could be writing. I know nothing about my father, nothing important, that is. I know the details, the dates and events of his life, the major and some of the minor characters, but I know as little about his inner life, his dreams, his desires, his disappointments, his little tragedies, as I do about my women. Less, in fact. For my women are complete, consummate, while Poppy is still unfinished. Unlikely as it may seem to anyone else, including himself, Poppy could still change, he could still come up with a surprise that would change the entire meaning of his life.

I wonder what that could be. I often can't sleep in North Bay and I sometimes entertain myself, while waiting for sleep, by speculating about what Poppy could do that would change not just his life but the *meaning* of it. If, for example, he dumped Virginia and ran off with the mistress, that would change his life, but it would have little effect on the meaning of it, he would still be basically the same person, living a conventional life—for what could be more conventional than leaving one's old alcoholic wife and running off with a woman the age of one's daughter? It's so common it's almost a cliché, simply another rite of passage for a certain type of middle-class male, just as being abandoned is simply another rite of passage for the women they leave behind.

If, on the other hand, he suddenly decided that all those years of handling his friends' divorces and getting their kids out of the drunk tank had been less than satisfying to his soul and he packed up and moved down south to devote his life to assuring voting rights for black sharecroppers or helping Haitian refugees fight the immigration system, that would change the meaning of his life.

I hate to think about it, because he is, after all, my own father, and I like to think of him as Good and Decent, but the truth is, he could just as easily go in the opposite direction, sell off everything he owns and buy a radio station and host a hate show, sitting in front of the microphone all day blaming all the country's problems on black sharecroppers and Haitian refugees and teenage mothers. That, too, would change the meaning of his life: at his death he would be a big demagogue in a little pond and everything he had done up to that point would have been in the service of it.

Virginia is as much a mystery to me as Poppy is, despite the fact that she's constantly trying to dump her life on me. "Tell me about the Geography Aunts," I used to plead as a child, finding the two old-maid aunts who raised her much more interesting than any fairy-tale witches, and she would sit on the side of my bed and tell me about her Aunts Florida and Asia, her mother's bitter sisters. She would lapse into her drawl, her voice soft and slow and enveloping, wrapping me up in her words, in her world. She would call herself "Ah!" with a little exclamation, as if she were surprised to find herself talking about herself, and I loved that, I loved that little note of wonder.

She talks about little else, now, and the soft, lilting "Ah!"'s of my childhood have been replaced by a hard, brittle, insistent "I." It is impossible to have a conversation with her without her turning everything around to herself—if Cease says something about his toys, she'll say, "*I* used to collect toys and I had one of those cast-iron banks with the jumping dog, I could just kick myself for throwing it at Florida and breaking it, it would be worth a fortune now," or if I say something about the book I'm working on, she'll say, "*I* could have been a writer too, you know, and I would have been just as good as you or your grandmother, but I got married and raised you instead." The less she does, the more she could have been, and it makes me want to strangle her.

"You do the same thing," my ex-shrink, Greta, pointed out, and I vowed to go back to my apartment and drown myself in the tub, but I didn't. I try to catch myself, but it's a disease, I suppose. "Narcissism," Greta said, and I stopped seeing her.

"Tell me about the Geography Aunts," I say when *Wheel of Fortune* is over, and Virginia triumphantly reenters the kitchen, flushed with her success.

"No," she says, "you'll steal them."

"Steal them?" I ask.

"You'll write about them," she says.

"But I thought you *wanted* me to write about your life," I say, wondering if she's trying a new tack, a little of the "reverse psychology" she claims she mastered me with as a child.

"I've decided I'm going to write a book about your grandmother," she says. "I'm going to ask your father to buy me a typewriter."

"Virginia, that's great!" I say, hoping she's too drunk to notice the phony edge to my voice, but she's not, she could catch it even if she were in a coma.

"Don't be patronizing," she says. "You don't think it's 'great' at all. *You* want to do it, you want everything for yourself, you think everybody's life belongs to you."

"If I'd wanted to write a book about Granny I would have already done it," I say. "She doesn't fit my *oeuvre*."

"Your *oeuvre*," Virginia sneers. "Your *oeuvre* is crap. Your *oeuvre* is crap and you are the most selfish human being on the face of the earth."

I don't see what one has to do with the other but she's drunk and she's determined to attack me, not because I've done anything, just because she needs to strike out and I'm the only available target. It's always been this way. "I may have humiliated you," Virginia always says when Cease begins carping about his lousy childhood, "but at least I never hit you."

She hit me instead. Not often and not hard, but every once in a while she'd come after me with a wet dishrag and begin lashing at me with it. It didn't hurt and she was usually so drunk she'd miss half the time, slapping the table or a chair or the banister as I ran upstairs to hide in the attic. I realized even then, even as a child, that it was somehow symbolic, her attacking me with that stupid rag, but I was never quite sure what it was symbolic of. Did she attack me because she felt like a wet dishrag and I reminded her of herself, being not only her namesake but also being almost twinlike in appearance, what with our white-blond hair and small, straight noses and lopsided smiles and large, bad teeth? Or was it because the dishrag was symbolic of the drudgery of housework to which she felt enslaved even though she didn't do it? Did my doing it for her make her feel so guilty she had to attack me? Or was it because she thought I liked the women on *Lady of Charm* better than I liked her and she was attacking me with the object she felt represented them? I never figured it out, and once, years later, when I first went into therapy and had to *know* everything, had to be *open* about everything, had to clear the air about everything, I asked her—I said, "Virginia, why did you always hit me with that dishrag?" and she said, "Hit you? I never hit you. That therapist must be putting ideas in your head," and that was the end of that. As far as she was concerned, she never had hit me, it was just something else I made up to torment her with. "I may be many things," she said, "but violent I'm not."

"You're not the only educated person in this household," she is saying. "I can write just as well as you."

"I'm sure you can," I say.

"And in any case, you get your talent from me, it came down in a straight line. Mother, me, you. I just haven't felt the need to express myself until now."

I feel panicked, even though I doubt she'll ever get any farther than dragging Granny's clippings out of the attic; Poppy will never get around to buying her a typewriter and she won't have the energy to go down to Peterson's and buy one herself. She'll come up with a thousand excuses as to why she can't get started even though no one cares whether she gets started or not.

Getting started wouldn't be too bad, it's what would happen when she started digging deeper than the surface that worries me.

"You just don't want any competition," she says. "That's why you write about those do-nothing women of yours. No one else *wants* to write about them."

"Or to read about them, either."

Poppy has emerged from his sanctuary, just in time for the punchline.

"Just kidding, Gingersnap," he says, coming over and tousling my hair. "Just a little joke."

"Cecil," Virginia says, "I want you to go to Peterson's tomorrow and get me a typewriter, and not one of those ones that beep all the time."

Poppy laughs. "They don't beep all the time, just when you make a mistake."

"Well, I don't want a machine that nags me. I want a regular typewriter, one that lets you make your mistakes in peace."

I tell her she can turn the Wordspell off, but no, that's too hard, she doesn't want to fiddle with it. "Just a regular one," she insists, "with no doodads."

"A doodad-less typewriter," Poppy says, giggling. "I don't know, that's a pretty tall order."

"Well, you can fill it," Virginia says, but he won't. He'll "forget." He'll "get busy" and it will "slip his mind."

Poppy retired years ago, but he still goes to the office every day, to read the papers and keep up to date on all the local lawsuits, to give unwanted advice and flirt with the secretaries. The firm still carries his name, even though there are no Moores in it, Cease having opted to be a bum rather than a lawyer. I suppose he used to slip away from the office in the afternoon to visit his mistress, whoever she may have been. I wonder if he still sees her, if she's someone we know, one of Virginia's former friends or the mother of someone I knew in high school, or, for that matter, a classmate. The idea makes me sick.

Poppy walks over to the sink and pours himself a glass of water. "Time for my medicine," he announces and pulls several vials from the windowsill, where they are lined up in rows, two deep, the left-hand sill for Poppy and the right-hand for Virginia.

Virginia rolls her eyes at me; she has always hated Poppy's habit of announcing every move he makes, even though she does it herself. "I'm going to take a shower now," or "Think I'll have a glass of juice," or "Guess I'd better go put some seed out for the birds." We all do it, it's an annoying family trait, one that drives Michael crazy. "Thank you for sharing," he always snarls when I tell him I'm going to the bathroom. "Number one or number two?"

Poppy rinses his glass and replaces it on the sink corner.

"Think I'll go up now," he says. "I'll let you girls talk."

He shuffles over to the table, as if taking the medicine has reminded him that he is old and infirm, and kisses Virginia on the cheek.

"Good to have you home, Ginger-ale," he says, tousling my hair again. "See you in the morning."

"He's got a new name for you," Virginia says after he leaves. "He's dying to use it but he's saving it for the right time."

"I can hardly wait," I say and Virginia laughs, for the first time since I arrived.

"He heard it on a commercial," she says, "and he's been waiting for just the right moment. He didn't think it would be as effective over the phone."

"Probably not," I say.

"I won't tell you what it is," she says. "I wouldn't want to spoil his fun."

Neither would I. Making up names for us is one of Poppy's greatest pleasures in life, his way of showing us how affectionate he is, and we endure them with relative good humor. Even Cease no longer cringes when Poppy calls him "Ceaseless" or "War and Cease."

"It would really hurt his feelings if you didn't laugh," she says. "You know how he is."

I know how he is. When we were growing up, there was only one way of thinking and that was Poppy's. No one dared to disagree with him, not because he'd rage but because he'd be so hurt. To have a thought unlike his was treason, betrayal, and when I was young I would try to stamp my own thoughts out, as if they were little brush fires in my brain, before they could burn with a passion that would scorch him. I'd run upstairs and crawl under my bed, the pain of disagreeing with him gnawing at my heart like a rat, as if I were killing him by having a thought of my own. And, in a way, it *was* a sort of murder. My own personality was trying to usurp his in my heart and mind and it was so unbearably painful I wanted to die.

"I'll laugh," I promise, and she says, "Good."

She gets up and heads for the liquor cupboard. "Think I'll go up, too," she says. "I'll just fix myself a little nightcap to take upstairs."

She glares at me while she fills her glass almost to the top with straight vodka, as if daring me to object, but we've all long since given up our objections, overruled, as Poppy used to say when he still admitted she had a "problem," by the force of her addiction.

"Good night, dear," she says.

"Good night, Virginia," I say and she disappears up the stairs.

5

THE DEAD, LIKE THE LIVING, OFTEN DISAPPOINT US BY TURN-
ing out to be other than we wanted them to be. But we still
have the option of avoiding the truth, ignoring it, keeping it
buried along with the disintegrating bones of our loved ones.

When I say "we" I don't mean biographers; *we* don't have
the luxury of avoiding the truth, at least not if we're any
good. If we come upon an unpleasant truth, we may choose
to portray it in a favorable light, or to bury it in a footnote, or
to interpret it in such a fashion that our subject appears to be
the hero rather than the villain, but we can't deny it. When I
say "we" I mean everybody else, including myself when I'm
not dealing with a subject. I'm just as capable as the next
person of shoving my head in the sand and keeping it there,
of clinging to a mythology more tolerable than reality, a
mythology, in fact, full of romance and beauty and adventure,

a mythology in which my grandmother, India Lee Currie, is the heroine, the goddess. Which makes us, her progeny, semi-immortal as well.

I wrap myself up in Virginia's heavy mink coat and head toward the beach. I have always been able to think more clearly on the beach, and Greta, were I still seeing her, would no doubt tell me that was because the beach is where the conscious meets the unconscious, which may well be true, but as far as I'm concerned it's because it's the only place where I know I won't be disturbed, where I won't meet anybody, for who in their right mind would sit on a cement breakwall in the dark, in subfreezing weather?

All the other houses in Edison Woods are gaily lit up for Christmas, the windows glowing with the warm yellow light of family gatherings, the driveways overflowing with cars with out-of-state license plates. Our house seems dark and abandoned, Scrooge-like by comparison.

When we were little, Edison Woods was a fairyland at Christmastime, everybody in the neighborhood would try to outdo everybody else with their decorations, and people would drive from as far away as Mount Clemens to gape at the Ditwells' twenty-foot waving Santa and the Pittsfields' Candy Land and the Prittles' life-sized crèche, complete with a real stuffed donkey. Mr. Peterson, Jr., who owned the local department store, had a movement-sensitive reindeer—very high-tech back in the dark ages of my childhood—that would light up and sing "Rudolph" whenever a car passed. The singing reindeer was a great hit with the neighborhood kids, and we'd sneak out in the middle of the night to ride our bikes back and forth in front of the Petersons', slipping and falling in the snow, laughing hysterically when Rudolph would light up and start singing, and Mr. Peterson, Jr., would run out in his polka-dot pajamas and shake his fist at us. "I know who you are!" he'd shout. "I'm going to call your parents!" and we'd shriek and scurry home, hoping the snow plow would bury the bike tracks leading to our respective garages.

Now, things are more subdued, a few strings of tiny white lights strung around a shrub or a small leafless tree, the reflection of the Christmas-tree lights in a window, a candle flickering behind a closed curtain, the faint sound of a carol playing on a stereo. Gone are the blaring PA speakers, the mechanical elves, the flapping wings of fat angels, and I can't say I miss them. What I miss is the wonder, the joy, the anticipation of a miracle.

Mine are the only footprints in the snow at the beach, undisturbed from this morning's walk along the shore. I follow them down to where the waves have begun freezing into ice mounds, "ice caves" we called them as children and Maggie Pittsfield and I would come down here and hide in them, with boxes of candy bars she'd stolen from her father's car, making up stories about ice monsters lurking far out on the lake from which we, with the help of our wonder dogs, Goober and Fritz, would save the town.

If there is one thing for which I will never forgive Virginia, it's Fritz. She murdered him. Had him put to sleep one day when I was at school, and all because he shit in her bedroom and she stepped in it. It's funny, I suppose—I can forgive her the beatings with the dishrag, the humiliation of having her show up at my friend's houses in her bathrobe, reeking of booze, of having to listen while the other kids sang songs about her: *"Mrs. Moore—can't find the door—she's passed out—upon the floor . . ."*

I can forgive her that and more: turning me into a scullery maid, making me quit Girl Scouts so I could keep her company while she sat in her rocking chair and endlessly wept, never saying a word, just weeping, louder and louder until I couldn't stand it anymore but I was trapped, trapped by pity and guilt and even, I suppose, love, although I didn't call it that, I thought all the love I had had for her was dead and all that was left was that god-awful pity.

It made me rather hard, I must say; I can't bear crying, not because I feel anything for the person who is hurt but because I think they want something from me, something I can't give, with every tear they shed they want a drop of my blood and I won't give it.

I can forgive her all those things because, in a sense, they had nothing to do with *me*. It wouldn't have mattered who was sitting there in the shade of the porch, as long as it was alive and human, and it was only me because I was the most convenient human being around. But killing Fritz, that was something else entirely. Fritz was *my* dog, I loved him with an irrational passion, I truly believed he knew and understood everything I said and that he loved me in return with—what else?—doglike devotion.

"When did he die?" Michael once asked when I was telling him a Fritz story and I said, "1962." "Jesus," he said, "you talk about that dog as if it died yesterday. Get a grip."

1962. An all-round lousy year. World War III would be avoided, but nothing could stop the destruction of our peaceful little world. Virginia had given up on Personhood and returned to Motherhood, giving birth to a son, whom they named Roger Ballentyne, in honor of the beloved father Virginia had barely known. I have a photograph, in New York, of myself, smiling and awestruck, holding little Roger in my arms, but I don't remember him at all, and if I didn't have the photo I would suspect him of being a figment of Virginia's imagination, just another excuse to get drunk, like Martha in *Who's Afraid of Virginia Woolf?* I don't remember her pregnancy, nor her giving birth. I don't remember ever holding him in my arms, which seems odd to me. As a child myself, he would have seemed to me like a living miracle, a wonderful round cuddly toy, a doll who would cry without my having to press a button, someone I could dress and feed and push around the neighborhood in a carriage. Sometimes I take out the photograph and try to bring forth some sort of feeling, some vague memory, but there's nothing, just a numb blank in my mind. He was there and he was gone, all within a few months, and then Virginia disappeared as well, never to return again, at least not as the mother I remembered. That woman was dead, dead and buried, and the woman who took her place was a hollow replica of Virginia, with nothing inside but need. Need, and an insatiable appetite for vodka.

The only good thing about that year was India. She swooped into our lives like some kind of flying behemoth with a southern accent, Dumbo in orange brocades and bright purple hair. She was going to save us, she was going to take care of Virginia, be the mother to her that she never had been, cure her with love, cover us all with a magical substance from her wizard's pot and glue us all back together.

She was everything a child could want in a grandmother— she was wild and funny and adventurous, she lived in Paris in an apartment overlooking the Seine, she attended grand balls where Charles de Gaulle himself would be present, she knew Camus and Sartre and de Beauvoir, names that meant nothing to me at the time except they sounded awfully romantic.

She too sounded as romantic as she looked, with her combination southern and French accents, with her *très*'s and her *mais oui*'s. But best of all, she could do magic tricks, she could make a quarter appear out of Cease's nose and turn an ordinary pencil into a candy bar. She seemed to know everything. She'd take us for walks in the woods behind our house and tell us how all the wildflowers got their names—bloodroots sprang up from the tears of a princess who had lost her way in the snow and every tear, as it touched the ground, turned into a drop of blood, which sank into the earth and reappeared in the spring as a tiny white flower and the trail of her flower-tears led her back home; touch-me-nots were little trolls who had angered the forest king by blowing up the bridge over his moat so he turned them into little yellow and orange flowers that exploded when touched. I took some touch-me-nots to school for show-and-tell and Mrs. Webster was appalled by Granny's stories but Granny said never mind, some people have no imagination.

"Imagination," she said, "is the greatest gift God can give you," but He must have given the family allotment to her, for none of the rest of us were blessed.

Another great thing about India's coming to stay with us was that I got to move out to the playhouse. At first, she slept in my room with me, which I considered a great honor, but she snored so loudly I couldn't sleep, so Poppy fixed me up a cot in my playhouse and I slept out there, away from India's snores and Virginia's sobs and Poppy's pleading and Cease's blaring record player. As soon as the streetlights would come on I'd call Fritz and kiss Poppy and Granny good night, Virginia, too, if she was still standing, and Fritz and I would escape out to the playhouse, to our own peaceful little world, behind the house and backing up to the woods, where the only sounds I'd hear were the cracking of branches as animals scampered around, scrounging for food, and the occasional questioning great horned owl, asking, "Hoo-hoo-hoo, who-who?" Sometimes I'd hear voices, too—some of the older boys would go in the woods at night and sit around looking at each other's penises, but I wasn't afraid because I had Fritz with me and even though he was only a dachshund, I knew he'd protect me. Besides, nothing at that point was more frightening than Virginia's hysteria.

In the morning, India would come out with a tray laden with pancakes and sausage and grits and we'd sit on the grass in front of the playhouse (she was much too large to get in) and she'd tell me about the children's park in the Tuileries while I ate and wished I could move to Paris with her.

She drove us to Detroit, to the zoo; she took us to Greenfield Village, where I would go in the settlers' houses and pretend to be a pioneer while Cease stood outside the window, whooping Indian war cries and waving a rubber tomahawk. She commandeered Mr. Peterson, Jr., and his yacht and we sailed across the lake to Canada, to Ipperwash, where Cease and I rolled down the great dunes and collected shells to take back to Virginia.

She'd force Virginia to get dressed, dressing her herself if necessary, and take her down to Grosse Pointe, to the very beautician who did Charlotte Ford's hair, and bring her back, groomed and made-up, looking enough like herself to give us a glimpse of the mother we'd lost, just enough to make us miss her even more when her hair became disheveled and the makeup ran in streaks from her tears and the new suit lay in a heap on her bedroom floor.

Having India around was such a delight I sometimes was glad Roger had died. I never knew what to do when those thoughts would start bouncing around in my head. I knew it was wrong and I thought I owed it to someone—Roger or God or Virginia or someone—to punish myself for having them and I'd lock myself in the bathroom and try to hurt myself, try to maim myself somehow, pull a handful of hair out by the roots or burn myself with Virginia's lighter or stick pins under my fingernails, but I could never do it, as much as I knew I deserved it, I couldn't hurt myself, and to make up for my cowardice I'd force myself to stay away from India for a day or two, deny myself the pleasure of her, the joy that had sparked off the bad thoughts in the first place.

As far as Virginia was concerned, India just made matters worse, but for the rest of us she was a godsend, larger than life and filled to capacity with it, bursting her wild brocades with an aliveness that filled the house so completely there was no room for sorrow, at least not for Cease and me. Poppy had already adjusted to his grief, filing it away in an outer chamber of his heart, where he placed all the little tragedies of his life, out of the way but accessible if necessary. Virginia was nothing but sorrow, sorrow and emptiness, and the more Granny filled the house with life, the less Virginia seemed to belong. We—Cease and I, and perhaps even Poppy—began to resent her, to cringe with loathing every time she emerged from her bedroom, half-dressed and half-crocked, screaming, "I killed him! I killed my baby!"

"Virginia Lee," Granny would say, "that is sheer and utter nonsense."

Virginia would stand in the doorway, crying and rubbing her hands and muttering. "I did," she'd moan, "I shook him to death," and Granny would tell her to stop playing Lady Macbeth.

"It doesn't become you," Granny would tell her. "Now, go to your room, get dressed, and behave."

She would, miraculously, get dressed, but she wouldn't behave, at least not the way any of us wanted her to, the way she used to. She'd come out of her room wearing a neat cropped suit or a chiffony cocktail dress and go lie on the porch swing and cry, rudely interrupting Granny's stories with her loud sobs and wet sniffles. In fact, they seemed to be a part of Granny's stories, a sort of punctuation, and when I discovered the truth about Granny, they seemed oddly appropriate.

6

MY LIFE IS MADE UP OF SHATTERED ILLUSIONS. AS A CHILD this was forced upon me, now it's my job.

It's not as though I go through life with a huge hat pin, gaily jabbing it into every bubble I pass. Illusion-bursting is, in fact, the part of my job I find most difficult, especially when the illusions are my own. But every life has its illusory portions, to a greater or lesser extent, and to do my job well I must sacrifice the fable, no matter how lovely, to the truth.

This is not as simple as it may seem. There are levels of truth. Facts are, after all, nothing more than facts—this and such happened at this and such time and place—they are amoral, unfeeling, as blind as Justice herself, they simply exist. It is our presentation of the facts, or, if you will, the truth, that places a value judgment on it. Facts themselves are lifeless, lying around like any other resource, and it is we who mine them and breathe meaning into them.

Take, for example, the European conquest of America. The native peoples lived here and had their own cultures, about which we know mainly from the Conquistadores and, more recently, from archaeologists. The Europeans came over in great numbers, killed off huge numbers of the native population, and then fought amongst themselves for the land. This we know. But what that *means* depends largely upon how that information is presented. History, as we know, is written by the victors and it's unlikely they're going to present themselves in an unfavorable light; therefore they must create an entire mythology to justify their actions and it is this mythology that eventually becomes "history." So, to the Europeans, the conquest of America means progress, the ascendancy of civilization, wealth, power, Manifest Destiny, while to the native peoples it means genocide, theft, and greed. To the Europeans, it meant a superior culture usurped an inferior one, while to the native peoples it just meant death. Facts don't know from "superior" or "inferior"; facts know nothing, they simply are.

Therefore, to me, being a biographer is a great responsibility. I'm constantly weighing the various facts of my subjects' lives against the *meaning* of it to decide how to present them without changing the meaning of that life, for I have no right to do that. Of course, it could be argued that the biographer has no right to assume he or she understands the meaning of the subject's life in the first place, and while that argument is valid, it's one I choose to ignore, for if I didn't I wouldn't get any work done.

It's our job, as biographers, to decide whether a certain truth is a footnote, a paragraph, a page, a chapter, or a book in itself, and that, needless to say, gives us a great deal of power. As with any kind of power, it can be exhilarating, but it also can be terrifying. I am always a bit in awe of my subjects, even when they prove to be irritating, intractable, disappointing, or downright awful. I'm still sensitive to the fact that I am holding a life in my hands and that my subject is as helpless as an infant, more so really, because an infant can at least cry out in objection to mishandling, while the dead can do nothing.

So, I try to shatter illusions carefully, although with my subjects it's unlikely that anyone besides myself and a few oddball scholars even knows there was anything to shatter, in fact I often have to re-create the myths in order to destroy them.

India's myth is another matter entirely. The illusions at stake don't belong to anybody out there in that vague, featureless mass we call "the public," they belong to my mother. And, to a lesser degree, Poppy and Cease, although Cease would probably be delighted to have another relative to add to his Dysfunctional Families game.

Virginia is right about my not being very enthusiastic about her attempting to write India's life, but she's right for the wrong reasons.

"You're always complaining I never *do* anything," she said, "and now, when I want to *do* something, you're trying to discourage me."

It's not, as she supposes, that I fear the consequences or begrudge her using material I may have use for in the future, although I suppose if I dug deep enough in my murky psyche I could find some dirty little seeds of resentment, as if I felt she were squandering my inheritance by using it herself, and yes, I suppose there's even some fear that she might actually do it, and do it well, and in fact prove herself "better" than I, but these fears are groundless, demonic delusions that have nothing to do with Virginia, that have to do solely with my sense of myself as a fraud.

I wish I could look into Virginia's heart and see what she wanted from India's life. Perhaps it wouldn't be such a disaster for her to discover that India wasn't the paragon we all thought her to be; in fact, it could be freeing. It all depends upon what Virginia needs from India, for her own sake, and frankly, I don't know Virginia well enough to say what that might be.

Every time I come to North Bay, I vow I will get to know my parents, but I never do. As long as they are my parents, they can't be people to me, they can't be individuals outside their respective roles, just as Cease and I can't be anything other than children to them. I am too close, the little failures of their lives, the tragedies, the losses, the disappointments, the acts of cowardice or malice, are unbearable to me. The pieces are too sharp, I can't hold them in my hand, nor can I paste them together into a picture of who they are. The pictures I've formed of my parents are lopsided, cubistic, abstract.

I hear the familiar thumpa-thumpa-thump of a freighter's engine and look up—there's a long, low ore carrier hurrying north to make it through the Soo before the locks close for the winter. It's too dark to make out the stack, but I guess it to be Cleveland Cliffs, more because I've always loved the name than from any telltale signs. The rails are garlanded with bright red and green Christmas lights and I wonder what the crew does for Christmas. I know they'll eat well— my ex-husband spent several summers shoveling coal in the belly of a freighter, and while he said he worked like a dog, he also said he ate like a king.

Michael doesn't believe that I was ever married. He thinks I made it up so I can pretend not to be an old maid, and to be honest about it, it was so long ago and I remember so little about it that I might as well have made it up. I have "proof," of course, I could dig out the wedding photographs and shove them in Michael's face but it wouldn't be worth it; he'd hoot and holler and fall around my apartment laughing when he saw me in my wedding gown, all 140 pounds of me, stuffed into a dress I bought when I weighed 110, looking like a sunburned piglet dressed up for the banquet table. That summer, while Frank was eating like a king on the freighter, I was eating like a hog at Farmer Bob's, sneaking into the back during my breaks and stuffing myself with whatever junk the stockboys had left lying around, shoveling it into my mouth like some kind of addict. It was horrible, but I couldn't stop, it was as if making myself fat was a duty, I had to be fat before Frank returned, to find out if he truly loved me, if he would still want to marry me when he came home and found me down at the lake, lying on my towel like a beached whale. Apparently he did, and I have the wedding photographs to prove it, but I'd rather Michael think me a liar than fat, so I leave the photos buried in a box full of college papers and letters, things I should just throw out but don't. That young woman no longer exists, but without the proof of who she was, I might forget her entirely. And who knows? She may prove to be important to the person I eventually become, the person I am at the end of my life, although I hope not.

I'm suddenly overwhelmed with a craving for potato chips and dip and I decide to go to Wally's. As I pass the Frasers' house I see a car there with Minnesota plates, a large old American boat of a car. Melanie must be home for the holidays and I think about stopping in, but there's no way of knowing whether she's on or off the wagon and if she's off I'd really rather not spend the evening listening to her blame me for having ruined her life. "You drank just as much as I did," she always says, "how come you're not a drunk?" and I don't know. I can't say, "Genes," because by all accounts I should be an alcoholic: my mother is, one of her aunts was and India may have been, two of my father's sisters were, and Cease is doing everything he can to make sure his portrait ends up on the wall with the family drunks. Melanie's family, on the other hand, is virtually drunkless, with the exception of Melanie herself. "At least I'm the first *something*," she says when she calls me up, pissed off and plastered. "Put that in your book."

"Ginger Moore!" Wally shouts as I shake the snow off Virginia's mink. "Where ya been, Chicago?"

I am stunned by how old Wally has become. Poppy told me he'd had a stroke, but I wasn't expecting to see him hunched over and wasted, half the man he was last year.

"Hey, Wally," I say, "what's news?"

His big, bellowing voice seems unreal, as if it were a recording coming out of the mouth of a waxwork figure, a sallow, sagging mold of the old Wally.

"Well," he says, shaking his bald shiny head, "I guess you heard about the Corwin boy."

I nod, although Derrick Corwin is anything but a boy, he was a year ahead of Cease at school, which would make him at least forty-two.

"I could've called that," Wally says. "He was always a no-good-nik. Even when you were kids, he was always in here stealing, and not like the rest of you little monsters, lifting a Tootsie Roll every once in a while, he *stole*. I caught him trying to open the till once and that was that, I called his mother and said, 'If I ever see that brat of yours in here again I'll have him put in The Home,' and Jean, you know, you couldn't find a nicer person, that was probably his problem, she was too nice, although she liked the sauce, too. Johnnie Walker, I think, Black. Anyway, he never came in here again, and not because of his mother. He'd always wait outside while his friends came in because he knew I meant it, if I saw that smirking mug of his on this side of the window, it'd be The Home for him, and so long, Charlie."

He leans against the counter, panting, and I tell him I heard Derrick was getting out. "I heard he found God in jail and was going to start a Christian motorcycle gang."

Wally lets out a howl and slaps the counter. "That's a good one!" he shouts. "Jerks for Jesus!"

Derrick Corwin is a bit more than a jerk; he nearly killed an FBI agent during a drug bust, but it's true, it's difficult to imagine him as a hardened criminal, he always seemed too goofy to be really mean, and who would have thought that that dim-witted, candy-stealing, water-tower-painting goofball would end up in Jackson? I would have guessed him to be more the drunk-tank type, keeping his badness local, restricting it to barroom brawls and driving into trees.

Some young people come in looking for champagne, and I walk around the store, gathering together goodies for my debauch, while Wally waits on them. There was a time when I knew everybody who walked through Wally's door, knew who they were and where they lived and what they did for a living, but North Bay has changed, the neighborhood has changed, and I am the outsider now. Not that it makes any difference, I always felt like an outsider even then, the only difference is that now the feeling matches the reality.

When the customers leave, Wally tells me he's read *The Obscure Muse*. "I thought it was real interesting," he says, vaguely, which either means he read it and hated it or he didn't read it at all, either of which is okay.

I stuff my booty in a bag and walk home, feeling guilty and decadent and undignified, thinking, "It's not too late. I could dump this stuff inside St. Thomas's back door," but I know I won't. I'll take it home and sit in front of the TV all night, watching old movies and stuffing myself with junk, feeling sorry for myself for being here, instead of in my own home, with my own children, decorating my own tree.

Whenever I come home, I behave like a twelve-year-old, down to my choices of junk food, and while I hate it, I can't help it. It's as if I discard my maturity at the back door, tossing it across the floor like a pair of soggy boots for Virginia to pick up, but of course picking up was never her thing, it was mine, and I'll dig my maturity back out of the pile when I leave, put it back on, and go home.

I walk along Iroquois Avenue, the western boundary of Edison Woods, and think about all the little tragedies contained in that small world. An eight-block square of the American Dream, fulfilled, perfect, everything exactly as it should be, and yet every third house contained a catastrophe of some sort, from minor ones, like ours, to major ones, like the Corwins'. It seemed out of proportion, too many disasters per square foot.

Perhaps it was the water; maybe those antifluoridation kooks had been right all along, tamper with your water and you court destruction. Or perhaps what we were taught, what we were led to believe, was wrong and life was not one happy occasion followed by another, success stacked upon success until perfection was attained, and all one had to do was work hard, be good, be disciplined, and not rock the boat. Edison Woods didn't prepare us for failure, for hardship, for suffering and unhappiness. Even the tiniest pebble in our paths seemed like a punishment from God for not having been good enough, not having worked hard enough, for having been less than deserving.

One would think I would have been immune to that, having grown up the way I did, but I wasn't. I just thought my life was a glitch, that mine was the only unhappy family in

Edison Woods, but judging from the number of my class-mates in jails, rehab, psychiatric hospitals, and cults, I guess we were just par for the course.

"Life is impossible," a professor of mine once said, and I think every household should have that hanging on the wall, stitched out on a sampler, next to HOME SWEET HOME and BECAUSE I'M THE MOM, THAT'S WHY.

Cease is home: Poppy's car is in the driveway, with no apparent dents, and I feel oddly resentful that I'll have to share my treats with him. I consider going out in the playhouse and hiding there until I've finished my feast but I know that's insane, I can always drive back to Wally's and get more, but that isn't the point. I am always amazed at how greedy I become when I'm here, how tenaciously I hold on to every crumb, and not just of food but of everything. Affection, love, attention—it's all up for grabs and we grasp every bit we can get and hold on to it like misers with their gold, hoarding it, hiding it away, and then bringing it out only in secret, to fondle and admire.

"Harvey called," Cease says when I walk into the kitchen. "I told him you were out screwing your ex-husband."

"Um," I say, "well, at least now he'll believe I was married."

I wonder what he wants. He certainly wants something, he isn't calling to wish me Happy Holidays. As far as I knew, he was flying back from L.A. to spend the holidays with Doris, the Other Other Woman, for in Michael's life we're all Other Women, his heart belonging, completely and unassailably, to Mommy.

Perhaps Doris gave him the boot again, or maybe he's in need of some new material. In any case, my holiday is ruined. Not that it was shaping up to be a particularly joyful one, but at least I would have been semi-sane. Now I'll spend the rest of the week fighting the compulsion to chain myself to the telephone, just in case, just in case, just in case the whim strikes him to call again.

I hate this. It's bad enough coming home and turning into a twelve-year-old, now I'll have to beat off the lovesick sixteen-year-old as well. There is no room for *me* inside myself, I feel as if I'll be obliterated by these silly wenches from my past.

"People who long for their youth are nuts," I tell Cease. "You couldn't pay me to go back even one year, not even one minute. I can't wait till I'm eighty."

"You *are* eighty," Cease says. "You've been eighty since the day you were born."

"Well, no wonder I can't wait to get there. It will be a relief to finally act my age."

Cease grunts and grabs the potato chips from my bag. Acting one's age has never been a big priority for him; he's been stuck at thirteen all his life and it seems he has every intention of remaining there forever.

"He sounds interesting to me," Michael says of Cease, but of course he'd sound interesting to Michael, to someone whose favorite pastime, besides screwing, is playing with his Gameboy. To me, Cease is just unbearably sad.

"Did you see anyone at Squeegee's?" I ask and Cease shakes his head.

"Just a bunch of kids," he says. "Everybody my age is dead or in AA."

"Maybe you should go to a meeting," I suggest and he glares at me.

"I'm never going into another basement as long as I live," he says. "I've had enough of hinge-heads for a lifetime."

I drop it. Sometimes I think Cease is determined to drink himself to death before Virginia does, to pay her back, a fitting punishment for her crime. It's the kind of spite-your-face logic that passes for common sense in our family, and

I've long since given up trying to correct it. It's not that I'm cynical; I'm just tired. "Why beat a dead horse?" Poppy asked one night, and that was the last he ever spoke of Virginia's "problem," at least in the present tense.

"Look what I found in my room," Cease says, pushing an old red notebook across the table at me. "Remember this?"

I open the cover. "How To Be A Moore" was scrawled across the first page, in my childish handwriting.

"Oh, God, Cease," I say, laughing, "where did you find this?"

"I just *told* you. In my room."

"I wonder if Poppy or Virginia have ever seen it," I say and Cease says he doubts it. "When was the last time she cleaned my room," he asks, "1960?"

"Re-mem-bah," I say, mimicking Virginia's drawl, "you ah a Mo-ah!"

"And so are fifty million other people!" Cease shouts, the refrain from our childhood. "There are seven million stories in the Naked City and half of them belong to Moores!"

"'Number six,'" I read. "'A proper Moore never leaves the house fully dressed.'"

"Read number twenty-two," Cease says. "That must have been yours—'A Moore never deigns to complete a sentence.' I've never used the word 'deign' in my life. You were always really pretentious."

"A Moore never responds to a petty insult," I say, and he says, "Where's that? I didn't see that one."

"How old were we when we did this?"

Cease shrugs. I can't remember either, although I do remember sitting huddled in the playroom, making up our list and giggling while Virginia danced around the living room with a broom. "The only time she ever used one," Cease used to say, "except as transportation."

I flip through the pages. "God, we were mean," I say. "'A

Moore always waits until all the guests are seated before throwing up on the main course.'"

"It's not mean," Cease says, "it's the truth. She *did* always wait until she had an audience before puking all over everything."

He's still furious. His fury is what keeps him going, all he has in life, besides his toys. To let go of it would create a vacuum, an emptiness so vast it would be unbearable, so he clings to it as if it were something of great value. I don't pretend to understand Cease's fury—it doesn't seem proportionate to the circumstances. Virginia's drunkenness and periodic craziness were an embarrassment to me, too, but I at least had my little friends, I had Poppy, I had the image of India, I had a life outside our home, populated with real people and the people I'd like to be. But Cease had no one. He had only his toys and his rage. He would furiously reject anything else, rebuffing the attempts at friendship the neighborhood kids would—generously, I thought—intermittently make, willfully turning himself into the outcast he wouldn't have otherwise been. He seemed determined to cut himself off from life, from anything that might give him pleasure or take his mind off his seething hatred. He had the air of a fanatic, a flagellant, constantly whipping not only himself but anybody or anything that came near him.

And, after all these years, he's still at it. Still pounding his way through life like one big fist, oblivious to what he's hitting, oblivious to the pain he causes anyone, even himself.

Or so I suppose. I've always thought I knew Cease because we shared a life, shared a childhood, but I don't know him at all. We haven't really talked since we were little, when we were best friends, inseparable buddies, comrades. And then suddenly he changed, he burrowed into himself and was lost to me. Huge chunks of his life are off-limits to me: I know nothing of his life now, nothing of his years in Vietnam, nothing of his life when he returned. We only share a history up to a point and after that he's as much a mystery to me as Poppy and Virginia.

"Your parents are still your primary relationship," Greta once said, and I was mortified, because it was true. Michael was out of my life at the time, and the only real relationship I had was with Sarah Fielding, Henry's sister.

They take up a lot of space, my parents, especially Virginia, and there isn't a lot of room left over for anyone else, at least not for anyone living, anyone who might need something from me. If it's true, as Virginia says, that I have no heart, it's because *she* has it. She took it when I was too little to fight for it, when, in fact, I wanted her to have it, when I would have given her anything she desired, my heart, my soul, my little life, if only she would love me again. I was too young to know I might need it back someday and so I let her have it and she hid it away and now neither of us knows where it is.

I toss the book back on the table and ask Cease if he's finished his Christmas shopping.

"I haven't got anything for *her*," he says, jerking his head toward the ceiling. Virginia's room is above the kitchen, and as children, we always whispered when we were in here, fearing she could hear our every word. If we so much as made a peep, she'd come running down the stairs, her bathrobe half open and her breasts, to our great shame, half showing, screaming, "You're talking about me!" Now we don't bother to keep our voices down, knowing she no longer cares what we say about her.

"What about Poppy?" I ask.

Cease grins happily. "Want to see?" he asks, eager as a child, and I nod. He runs upstairs and returns with a beautiful blue-green parrot in an ornate cage and a small remote control device.

He places it on the table and then pushes the remote control. The parrot's head nods up and down and he says, in Poppy's voice, "How about a game of Monopoly?"

It's hilarious. Cease punches another button and the parrot says, "Time for my medicine!" "Guess I'll go up now!" "What's for dinner?" "Better get a move on!"

We sit at the table, laughing at Poppy's voice coming from the pop-eyed bird. Cease is delighted with himself, as well he should be, he's a genius when it comes to toys. It's just in every other aspect of his life that he's a nincompoop. Or seems to be. We are none of us what anyone would call well-balanced, it's just that Poppy and I are lopsided in ways that are less noticeable. Or seem to be.

7

"MY GIRLFRIEND'S A SCHIZOPHRENIC," MICHAEL SAYS IN
one of his bits. "Half the time she's a regular person and half
the time she's a Scholar. I never know whether I'm going to
get her or the Mad Professor, a normal human being or"—
and here he hums the theme from *The Twilight Zone: ne-*ne-
ne-ne—"The Creature from the Ivory Tower."

I'm not as bad as he makes me out to be. My eyes don't
glaze over and I don't start speaking in a pseudo-British accent, as if my mouth were filled with gumballs. And I certainly don't turn into a pretentious little automaton, making
even the most mundane comment sound like a lecture.

"I go to bed with my girlfriend," he continues, "and wake
up with Alistair Cooke."

It's true, I do become another person when I'm working,
but it's only because I have to. I don't feel that the person I

am naturally is equipped to do the work I've set out to do; she is neither intelligent, imaginative, nor patient enough to do serious work—she is, in fact, a silly, impressionable, giggly goose, the girl Mr. Hegley told to forget about college and make babies instead. She could never possibly know everything she needs to know in order to attempt to write a biography, to make sense of a life, to, God forbid, have an opinion. She's impressionable. She lacks wisdom. And so I try to be someone else; I try to be what I imagine a biographer to be: serious, dignified, thoughtful, slightly dowdy perhaps, not because of an inherent lack of style but rather out of absentmindedness, a person who lives in the black and white of the past rather than the Technicolor of the present or the neon of the future.

God only knows what I would have become if I hadn't developed an alter ego. "A person," Michael suggests, "a person with a head and a heart in the same body."

I always point out that what I change is my attitude, not my body, but he doesn't understand. I tell him that all I am doing is making a conscious effort to do what most men can do without even thinking about it, to change from living my life through my heart to maneuvering in the world with my head, but he is determined to think of me as some kind of Jekyll-Hyde monster, mutating into a hunched-over, pinched-faced, dust-covered old hag, a joyless old crow cawing over my dead carcasses.

The irony is, my "dead carcasses" give me a great deal of pleasure, they give meaning and purpose to my life. With every truth I discover about my subjects, I discover a truth about myself, about life in general, about what it means to be a human being, and the living don't give me that. The living are confusing and chaotic, bewildering, changing as rapidly as the world we live in. Every time I think I've got ahold of them, that I've discovered something solid in them, they dissolve into something else, slip through my fingers, and the only truth I'm left with is that I know nothing.

I find that intolerable. I need something solid in my life and I suppose if I hadn't become a biographer I probably would have joined a cult, shaved my head and run through the streets in a sheet, banging on a drum or shaking a tambourine, all in the hope that whatever it was I believed in was real. But I have no faith, and that's something one can't manufacture with a change of attitude, at least not if it's real. It takes an act of grace to believe in anything—God, justice, the inherent goodness of humanity, science, oneself, Progress with a capital P, anything. The only thing I believe in is truth and even that is beyond me. I believe in it, but I don't believe in my ability to grasp it.

It seems as though my whole life is nothing but a history of lies, but I can't be sure. I don't really remember life B.V.B.—before Virginia's breakdown—or, more accurately, I don't know if what I remember, which is lovely and idyllic, is real or just another lie, a lie I told myself so I could hope to return to it, a kind of personal Return to the Garden myth to make my life livable. There is evidence to suggest that my memories *are* real: photographs, jerky, sputtering home movies, Poppy's stories, but I can't be sure they're representative of life B.V.B. or simply the aberrations upon which we built our mythology.

"Ginger!" Poppy calls from the bottom of the stairs. "Gingerbread girl! Rise and shine! Up and at 'em!"

I grope for my plastic alarm clock and try to make out the time but it's too dark, too dark to be anywhere near dawn.

"Cease and Desist!" he shouts. "Get a move on!"

Cease responds with a thud, either falling out of bed or throwing something at the door, who knows, the only thing one can be sure of with Cease is that he will be hung over and surly.

I grab my bathrobe and make a run for the bathroom, to claim it before Cease does, but I'm too slow, he surges forth from his bedroom with a reeking blast, pushes me aside, and slams the bathroom door in my face.

"Nyah-nyah," he says as he whacks the toilet seat against the tank.

I trudge downstairs, furious that I have to use the downstairs bathroom, an afterthought to the house, added to a corner next to the porch, as cold as an outhouse. We all hate it and will fight like rats to get the upstairs bathroom, where it's warm and cozy. I have always lost.

"I made breakfast!" Poppy announces proudly as I enter the kitchen, thrusting a bowl of watery oatmeal at me.

"Thanks," I say, wishing I didn't have to eat it, but Poppy would be crushed if I rejected his offering so I swallow it down, trying not to gag.

Cease is not as polite. "I'm not eating that shit," he sneers, stomping over to the refrigerator and pulling out last night's steak, grabbing a bone and gnawing at it while he glares at Poppy and me.

"You kids all set?" Poppy asks.

"Yeah," Cease growls, shuffling over to the table and collapsing in a chair, "I always chop down Christmas trees in my skivvies."

Poppy giggles. This is the highlight of the season for him, the annual trek out to Abbot's to get the tree. We always have to start out before dawn, to get there and get the tree and get back before Virginia is up, to "surprise" her, although after thirty years it isn't much of a surprise.

"I don't know why we have to get up so early," Cease says. "She doesn't wake up till noon anyway."

I kick him under the table. We do it because it's important to Poppy, not to Virginia. Virginia doesn't care about Christmas or anything else. "Let's just skip it," she says every year, and that would be fine with me, it would save me the annual white-knuckle drive through Canada, in a blizzard, with semis thundering past on both sides while I try to keep my little tin-can car within the ruts of slush, but it would break Poppy's heart.

"Come on, come on," Poppy says. "Time's a wastin'."

He's ready. He's got on his "work pants," the pants he bought himself at the Pro Shop one summer—beige background with little green hunting scenes, little tapestry-like squares running up and down his legs. "The allegorical pants," Virginia calls them. "He thinks he's natty," she always says and she was thrilled when the knees ripped out of them, tore the galloping horse right in two. But Poppy refused to part with them, they were his, the pants he had picked out, by himself, without his wife tagging along insinuating he had no taste, no style. Perhaps they were a bit shabby for the club, he said, but they were perfect for tree-cutting, and he patched them himself, making long green stitches across the beheaded horse, Dr. Frankenstein bringing horse and rider back to life, a new life out at Abbot's Tree Farm, where Floyd Abbot would always chuckle and say, "Tally ho!" as he handed Poppy a chain saw.

Virginia's awake; the smell of her cigarette greets me at the top of the stairs, but part of the game is pretending she's asleep, off in some happy dreamland, from which she will awaken to find another dreamland, downstairs in the den, where her TV used to be. That too is part of the annual drama: Virginia grumbles about having to "adjust her eyes" to the TV in its temporary home in the kitchen, or the living room, she doesn't understand why Poppy can't put the tree somewhere else, what's wrong with the living room, why doesn't he move the tree instead of the TV? But the tree has always been in the corner of the den and that's where it will always be, TV or no TV. The happiest part of Christmas,

Virginia says, is tossing the tree out with the trash and getting back to normal.

I rifle through the dresser for my own tree-cutting ensemble: a pair of old flannel-lined jeans and a moth-eaten set of long underwear. Every time I come home, there are fewer of my things in the dresser, replaced by odds and ends of Virginia's—the needlepoint grids she never used, the purses she was going to découpage, the yarn for sweaters she was going to knit, the seeds for flowers she was going to grow. It's as if she's trying to get rid of my memory, tossing out little pieces of me, bit by bit, so there's less of myself to connect with every time I come here. Cease's room, on the other hand, remains untouched, with every dustball in place from his youth, every mouse turd lying undisturbed under his bed.

Poppy's head appears in my doorway. He's grinning wildly.

"Ginger," he says.

"Yesss?" I ask, suspicious.

"Ginger-vitis!" he shouts and bursts out laughing at his joke and I laugh dutifully; he's been waiting a long time for that one, saving it up until he could see my face and I reward him with a happy smile. He grins merrily and trots away, telling me to hurry up, we don't want to be late.

"No, no, a thousand times no," I said when Michael started talking about having children. Unfortunately, Michael uses that as a handy excuse every time he wants to run back to Doris, who *does* want to have children, and he stays with her until she gets serious about it. As soon as she starts talking about throwing away the birth control, he grabs his box of condoms and heads back across town, until I too get serious, serious period, until I fall into what he calls my "Germanic mode." "You're too intense," he says and flees back across the park.

Although I often wonder what Michael is doing with me, it rarely occurs to me to wonder what I'm doing with him, although I suppose I should. We are not exactly what anyone would call a "match." I am studious and serious and generally depressed; Michael is, well, he's a stand-up comic. He's irreverent and hyperactive and manic. "Together we make a whole human being," he says, and I guess that's part of the attraction. Michael certainly gives my life an edgy quality it wouldn't otherwise have. And one doesn't need a psychiatrist to see that Michael fills a certain need on my part, over and above the obvious ones—the need to be seen, to be visible, to be standing and sweating in front of the footlights, sucking in a roomful of attention rather than shivering in the archives, behind the scenes, drab and unknown. He gives me access to a world I wouldn't otherwise know, the downtown world of comics and musicians and actors, a world where everyone dresses in black and says "fuck" a lot, where everyone is young and alive and utterly engrossed in their little pocket of life.

It was in London that I first met Michael, during the depression I sank into after my discovery of Angeline Wilton's novel. I was lonely and broke and discouraged and homesick; I felt every bit the alien I was and I decided I needed something American—a hamburger, an evening of jazz, a basketball game, anything. What I found was Michael.

I'd been leafing through a *Time Out,* searching, actually, for a bar with a satellite dish where I could watch the Pistons in the playoffs, when I came across a review of this "bitingly witty" American comedian who "skewered" American culture. The old saw about absence making the heart grow fonder is true for countries as well as persons—the longer I stayed away, the more homesick I became, and the more homesick I became the less irritating America's flaws seemed, in fact they seemed rather benign, almost endearing, I began to see America as some sort of gangly adolescent, a kind of ill-mannered, untaught, unsophisticated Baby Huey, too huge and too powerful for his own good, but basically well-meaning. Well, I thought, why not, having it "skewered" is better than not having it at all, and I searched through my purse for a few 10p coins for the bathtub and braved my way through the freezing hall to get cleaned up.

I almost didn't make it. At one point, while sitting in the train heading for Islington, I looked up from my book and saw myself reflected back in the dark window opposite, looking horribly pathetic and sad, as if I had NEEDY scrawled across my forehead in black ashes. I nearly got off the train at the next stop to turn around and return to my forlorn bedsit, but what was *there*? Three boxes of notes and *The Abduction of Abigail*, half a pack of Digestives and a flat Tab, the humiliating memories of my silly dreams, and the Panel of Judges, buzzing around the room like a pack of nasty little mosquitoes, camouflaging themselves in the ugly brown flowers on the wallpaper, waiting for me to return so they could start sucking my blood again.

Virginia kept me on the train. As I sat there, debating what to do, I heard her voice, as clearly as if she were sitting right next to me. "Never go anywhere alone," she said. "It makes people think no one wants you."

My mother had been telling me that for as long as I could remember, and although I had long since come to the conclusion that "people" didn't give a shit whether you were dead or alive, much less whether or not anyone else "wanted" you, it was still a difficult phobia to overcome. What made it especially irritating to me was that it wasn't even my own phobia, it was hers, and it infuriated me that I had to waste my time grappling with a fear that, left to myself, I wouldn't even have.

The minute I walked into the club, however, my spirits rose. For one thing, it was warm, which was more than I could say for any other place I'd been in the past six months, it was warm and crowded and smoky and incredibly loud. I had forgotten how loud the living are, and although I normally detest noise of any sort, I was so tired of listening to the whispers of the dead that the racket of the club seemed wonderful, embracing, as if someone were throwing a party to welcome me back to the land of the living.

I shared a table with three young men from Amsterdam, all named Ian, who were backpacking their way through Europe after having successfully weaseled their way out of compulsory military service. Ian I had faked bad eyesight; Ian II had his doctor exaggerate his slight allergy to wool; and Ian III, my favorite, had spent his first night at boot camp crying so pitifully for his mommy that they sent him home.

The three Ians were so entertaining that I was somewhat disappointed when the lights dimmed and the owner of the club climbed up on the little plywood platform to introduce Michael. The crowd was happy, expectant, eager to be amused, and I thought, "This guy would have to be a moron not to please this audience."

He wasn't a moron but he wasn't very good either, at least in my opinion, although everyone else seemed to enjoy him. He was trying to be a combination Lenny Bruce and Richard Pryor, but he wasn't obsessed and he wasn't black; he was neither kinetic nor plastic; he had neither the urgency nor the vulnerability which made Bruce and Pryor great. What he said was biting, in the mean sense, but there was no danger there, no feeling that he, or by association we, could get in trouble for any of this. Portraying Americans as a bunch of fat, beer-drinking, TV-watching, peanut-eating (Carter was president at the time and for some reason peanuts became hilarious), fad-obsessed idiots to an audience that already loved to hate us was just too easy.

Being completely humorless myself, I have a great admiration for funny people, but I'm also a severe critic. There is not nearly enough laughter in my life and I am always tremendously grateful when someone brings some in, like Ian III, scrunching up his face and howling, "MOMMY! I WANT MY MOMMY!" Now *that* was funny. It was funny because it was about *him*. Michael, on the other hand, made fun of pet rocks and Billy Beer and *The Dating Game,* things I found pathetic rather than funny. Real humor, I find, makes fun of one's own vulnerability rather than someone else's.

I told him so. It was the disappointment over my work that made me so bold, that and the fact that the Ians had bought me more than a few beers. I normally would never dream of assaulting a performer with an unsolicited critique, but emboldened by drink and despair, I wobbled up to the bar, where Michael was standing, surrounded by adoring miniskirted girls, and said, "Excuse me, but don't you think you'd be funnier if you put yourself on the line a little bit?"

"Fuck you," he said and I wobbled back to the Ians, followed by the girls' appreciative shrieking, thinking that would be the last I would ever see of Michael McElroy, but I was as wrong about that as I had been about Angeline. About an hour later the miniskirts disappeared and Michael came over to our table. It wasn't what I had said that interested him, he told me, it was my voice—Michael, it turned out, was as homesick as I was.

We had to walk back to my bed-sit, the trains and buses having stopped running for the night and neither of us having enough money for a taxi. From Islington to Maida Vale is quite a hike, long enough, if nothing else, to get to know the person you're walking with well enough to decide whether to shake hands at the door or let them in.

He was charming and smart and much funnier in person than on stage. "When I was a kid," he told me, "I had this hearing thing: I couldn't understand anything anybody said. I thought 'Fifty-four forty or fight' was 'Fifty-four Morties tonight.' Every time I got up to recite something everybody would start peeing their pants laughing; when it was my turn to lead the class in the Pledge of Allegiance the teacher would have to leave the room to keep from laughing. It didn't take long to figure out that making people laugh was more important than getting things right, and even after I had an operation and could hear fine I still fucked everything up, just to get a laugh.

"There's nothing like it, making people laugh," he said as we sat down on a cold bench in Regent's Park. "It's better than drugs, better than sex, even." He paused and looked at me. "Well, as good as sex. As good as really great sex. As good as the greatest sex you've ever had, that's how good it is."

I couldn't imagine, never having had any "really great sex" myself. It was yet another thing I worried about—sex, to me, could be many things: fun, exciting, pleasurable, even transporting, but it wasn't anything I'd go to war over. I just didn't understand the obsession with it, I didn't understand why some people could be driven to murder, embezzlement, blackmail, insanity by it. The worst thing I had ever done in the midst of a lust craze was to go on a wild underwear-buying spree, charging hundreds of dollars' worth of lace and satin bras and panties. But obviously, for so many people to be so incredibly driven by it, there must be something extraordinary I was missing, and that was probably my fault, I was probably one of those dead fish men joke about, I was probably as cold and heartless as Virginia said, I was probably frigid.

Under normal circumstances I would have just nodded and said, "Mmmm, yeah, great sex, I know what you mean," pretending, as I often do, that I understand what I assume everyone else understands, trying to cover up what I fear is some sort of disability, hoping no one will discover that there's something "wrong" with me. But that night, for some reason, I felt I had nothing to lose, I knew I'd never see Michael again and I felt rather contentious, so I said, "Just what *is* great sex?"

He was shocked. "What do you mean?" he asked.

"I mean, what *is* it? Multiple orgasms? Feats of endurance, twenty days in the sack or something, flying off to Never-Never Land, what?"

"Well, if you don't know, I can't tell you . . ." he said and I stood up.

"I hate that," I said, and he said, "What? What's the matter?"

"I just hate it when I ask a perfectly reasonable question and someone answers by inferring that there's something wrong with me for not already knowing the answer, as if there's some kind of Great Sex Club and I'm not good enough to join it."

"Jesus," he said, "you're intense enough to join it."

"I don't want to join it," I said. "I'm going home."

"Can I come?" he asked and I shrugged.

"Are you always so intense?" he asked and I shrugged again. The truth is, I am, but it's been my experience that intensity tends to scare people off, it's a paradoxical effect, the same intensity that attracts them in the first place makes them run like hell later. My best friend, Cassie, says it's like anything hot, anything that burns, one is initially attracted by the warmth but there's always the fear that it might get out of control.

As it turned out, by the time we got to my bed-sit I decided I liked him again. He took a look around and did a pretty fair Bette Davis "What a dump" imitation and we had what I considered to be pretty mediocre sex, but what do I know? "*This* will be the end of Michael McElroy," I thought, but I was wrong again: he showed up the next night, and the night after that, and every night until his gig was over and he flew back to the States.

The sex still wasn't "great," but it was fine, it was fun, I enjoyed it tremendously, but what I really enjoyed was Michael's company. During the day, when I should have been at the library, we explored London, I took him to all the obscure little museums I had discovered where ancient gray men in dusty tweed jackets led us through rooms filled with bizarre collections, and to the Sir John Soane Museum, where Hogarth's *A Rake's Progress* hangs. I showed him the detail in the tavern scene, where down in the corner, one of the drunks is playing "Mr. Hand," with a little face painted on his fingers, and told him how, whenever I felt depressed, I would come and look at that and feel wonderfully silly and happy again. We went to the London Dungeon, where Michael couldn't get enough of Anne Boleyn's beheading. On Sunday, we went to Speaker's Corner in Hyde Park and Michael got up on an overturned trash can and ranted nonsense for an hour, drawing a considerable crowd, and I stood off to the side, laughing with delight and falling in love.

When he left, I felt bereft. Even though the sex hadn't been anything I'd kill myself over, I did manage to devolve into an obsession, a horrible, time-eating, life-sucking, misery-making obsession, the kind of obsession only a sixteen-year-old is equipped to handle—having nothing better to do, they can afford to lose a few months of their lives mooning and singing love songs.

It was horrible. To find myself, at twenty-seven, filling entire notebooks with Michael's and my names, trying to make them "work out," not even remembering from my schoolgirl days what "working out" was—was it giving the letters numerical values and getting them to add up to the same number? Or was it crossing out all the matching letters and trying to make the number of letters come out the same? Was one supposed to add the double digits to make single digits? It didn't matter. Hard as I tried, I couldn't make our names "work out" to anything other than a humiliating pile of crumpled paper.

I had only two months left in London and I was in danger of wasting them both doing nothing but wandering the streets, retracing our steps, standing outside the museums we'd visited together like some forlorn and discarded waif. It was ridiculous. The Judges chided me for having watched too many forties movies, for expecting, hoping, that my shipboard romance could be anything other than what it was—a happy little fling, no more, no less.

I was, I admit, lust-driven, not because I was in love with Michael—I barely knew him—nor because the sex was so unbelievably great, but because it was the only sex, the only companionship, the only human closeness I had experienced in a very long time. The lust wasn't so much for his body but rather for his presence, and after ten days of intimacy, no matter how superficial, I wanted more. Anyone who has ever been lust-driven knows that when the obsession sets in, the brain is the first thing to go, which is of course exactly why the American media are so fixated on sex and obsession. It's a plot, a plot to keep the American people stupid and pliable and unthinking, driven by lust, perfect little consumers and bad little democrats, for who cares about anything so boring as politics or economics or education when one is gripped with lust?

I love conspiracy theories. I was born at the height of McCarthyism; the notion that there was an evil "They" out there somewhere was a part of the very air I breathed and it entered my unformed and receptive little consciousness un-filtered by common sense or reason. It was just there, this big ugly blob of fear and distrust, seeping into any receptacle that was available, and there I was, a child, ready to take in any-thing the world would give me. What it gave me was para-noia. I'm not alone in this, of course, there were millions of us nourished on fear and suspicion, which is why we're currently being inundated with all sorts of conspiracy theories. From the right, from the left, from everywhere in between including outer space. And so whenever my life gets out of hand, when I'm unable to control my feelings or thoughts or behavior, I blame it on "Them," those Bad Guys out there who want to turn me into a Pod Person, a faddist, running after whatever is newest, hottest, sexiest, driven by the craziest logic imaginable, if one had the sense to be logical about it, which is to rise above the crowd by being part of it.

"You're out of your mind," Virginia says, and she may be right, but crazy or not, it works for me. Invariably, my anger at "Them" for trying to keep me in that distressing, undignified, hysterical state is enough to get me out of it. I went to bed one night ranting about "Them" and awakened the next morning with the realization that Angeline was in fact the true author of *Landymere* and *Manfred*. That was that; Angeline reclaimed her position in my mind, nudging Michael out, becoming more alive as he began to fade into my own history.

I thought about him occasionally, and when I moved to New York I went to see him perform downtown, in a ratty little club on the Lower East Side where the men wore more makeup than the women. When he came on stage, I was devastated. It was as if I was being engulfed by his presence, wiped out, and, much to my horror, that was precisely what I wanted. All my striving, my ambition, my hard work, were just gone, vaporized, and I was overwhelmed with a sense of relief, of having been relieved of a burden too huge for me to carry. It was, I suppose, similar to having a certain kind of religious experience, in which one is suddenly released from the responsibility of living. For the first time in my life I felt unselfconscious; I was there, I was aware of everything going on around me, but it didn't have anything to do with *me,* nor

I with it. I didn't have to *do* anything, I felt light and wonderful and free. "Great sex" be damned, *this* was what I wanted from Michael, and I've spent the past eight years trying to get it back.

"What are you doing up there?" Poppy cries from the bottom of the stairs. "Let's get a move on. The early bird gets the tree!"

"Okay, okay," I yell, "I'm just getting dressed."

Every year, Poppy seems a little more dotty, a little less like the brilliant lawyer I worshipped in my youth. He was the smartest father in town, he knew everything, he was Clarence Darrow and William Jennings Bryan rolled up into one, he was as wise as Solomon and as hilarious as Soupy Sales. He could have been president, I proudly told all my friends, but he wanted to stay in North Bay, with us.

The truth of the matter is, Poppy was always a bit of a goofball, although I don't remember his being quite so silly. Or perhaps he was and I just wasn't so serious, perhaps what seems like dotage now seemed like high comedy then. And perhaps if I weren't so "Germanic" I wouldn't even mind.

Not that I do mind, terribly. It's just sad to see someone who was once erudite and articulate reduced to making joke names out of gum diseases. He reminds me of Archie Rice in *The Entertainer*, except he's not quite as tragic as Archie, he has everything he wants, he is, as he will tell anyone who will listen, "the happiest man in North Bay." All his tragedies are behind him, except the big one, and at the rate he's going with his "memoirs" it's unlikely he'll ever have to relive any of them.

8

I DID NOT ALWAYS WANT TO BE A BIOGRAPHER. WHAT I DID
want, as far back as I can remember, was to be someone else,
and not just one "someone else" but many someone elses. I
wanted an opportunity to try on many different lives, to go
back in history and jump into the future, to be a pioneer, a
medieval princess, a Greek warrior, a heretic, a revolutionary,
a space traveler, a scientist. I especially wanted to be a martyr
(as long as there was no pain involved in my death), dying
valiantly for what was Right and True.

What I wanted, and I cringe to say it, it's so embarrassing,
was to be an actress. I didn't just want to be these things in
my mind, which was relatively easy to do, even for someone
as unimaginative as myself. I wanted to *be* Laura Ingalls
Wilder; I wanted to put on a calico dress and a white bib
apron and live in a sod house and bravely endure the hard-

ships God dished out, one after another. I wanted to feel what the world *felt* like to her, I wanted to immerse myself so completely in her, in her world, that Ginger Moore no longer existed—poof, she was gone, obliterated, at least for a while, at least as long as she was wearing the clothes of another person, of another time.

I never pursued it, of course, being an actress was something far too grand for me. One had to be pretty and popular and gregarious and full of confidence in order to be an actress, and I was none of the above. I wasn't nearly as ugly as I thought myself to be, and under other circumstances I might even have found my unusual looks a source of pride rather than of shame. But the circumstances were what they were, and I grew up wishing technology would move a little faster, fast enough to get to the point where I could have a head transplant. I would lie in bed at night, thinking about the head I'd choose, going through lists of all the famous dark-haired actresses of the time, for the last thing I wanted was to be was blond, being blond was my problem. I was too blond, too white, too pale, too colorless. "The Albino," they called me at school, and even though I tried to tell them that real albinos have pink eyes, they wouldn't listen, I was the closest thing they'd ever seen to an albino and that was good enough for them.

There was nothing wrong with my features, except my teeth, which were too big for my mouth, but I planned to have them all pulled as soon as I was sixteen, to have them all pulled and replaced with nice neat symmetrical rows, like white corn. While other children would drift off to sleep with images of soft sheep happily jumping over fences, I would imagine myself in a roomful of bodiless dark-haired heads, ticking them off one by one until I finally fell asleep. After much debate, I narrowed my choices down to Katharine Hepburn and Natalie Wood, reluctantly discarding Ingrid

Bergman, whom I considered to be the most beautiful woman in the world, because she was too close to blond, she might even *be* blond—who could tell in those black-and-white movies—and she was, after all, a Scandinavian of some sort. I finally decided I wanted Natalie Wood's head because she was young enough that it wouldn't look funny on my body, and I would slowly fall asleep, thinking about how different my life would be if only I could just change heads with her.

It wasn't until college that I realized, while researching a paper on *Frankenstein,* that there was another way. That by immersing myself in someone else's life, in her time and place, in her world, I could become not her, not Mary Shelley, but someone else, not myself, not Virginia Moore, Jr., not Ginger-ale, but a new person, a person different from the one Virginia wanted and the one I thought I had to be.

It was paradoxical but true—I only felt like myself when I was immersed in someone else's life, when I was sitting in the parlor with Mary and Percy and Byron, a fly on the mantelpiece above the blazing fire, listening with rapture while they told ghost stories. I would become obsessed: I had to know what Mary Shelley wore, what her shoes looked like, what color her drapes were, where she kept her chamber pot. Needless to say, the person who wrote *Frankenstein* must have had an interesting relationship with her parents (her father, actually, her mother having died giving birth to her) and that, in fact, was the theme of my paper, that parents-to-be should throw out their Dr. Spocks and read *Frankenstein* instead. For in addition to everything else that it is and was, it's a brilliant case study of how *not* to raise a child, of how, on the contrary, to assure that the being you've brought into the world will turn out to be a monster. So of course I had to know everything about William Godwin and Mary Wollstonecraft.

I'm still working on my Mary Shelley biography; it is to be

the culmination of my work, my magnum opus. Mary Shelley is the exact opposite of my shadowy women, my pale paraplegics; she was a woman who was surrounded on every side by larger-than-life figures, and instead of fading in their brilliance she shined ever-brighter, eventually eclipsing them all. For, while it may be true that most everyone has *heard* of Percy and Byron, how many people do you know who have actually read *Prometheus Unbound* or *Childe Harold?* Who remembers William Godwin? Mary Wollstonecraft is kept alive by feminists, but it's unlikely anyone will ever make a movie based on *The Vindication of the Rights of Woman.*

Mary Shelley could *do.* When I've finished with my women who couldn't, I want to explore the life of a woman who could, to see if there is something she had that the others lacked, or something she didn't have, some burden she didn't have to contend with, that they carried around, weighing them down to the point where they could no longer move.

The truth of the matter is, I'm not ready for Mary. The women I've written about up to this point have been my equals; they were women I could comfortably inhabit, I understand their fears, their neuroses, their insecurities. But Mary, I'm afraid, is too huge for me; I'm afraid she's too smart for me, or that I am too stupid for her, that I will climb inside her and be completely baffled, overwhelmed not in the way I desire but rather by my own inadequacy. I am terrified that the maze of her life and her mind is one I can't possibly find my way out of, much less elucidate.

Cease pounds on my door. "Let's get this over with," he growls and I pull on my old fisherman's sweater and run downstairs.

We all reek of mothballs. It seems insane that we keep these tattered, smelly rags to wear once a year but Poppy insists everything be the same; he's like a three-year-old who thinks Santa won't come if we don't leave exactly the same treats in exactly the same spot, the way it's always been.

There are no other cars on the road, which is a good thing, because Poppy is the world's worst driver, putting along at ten miles an hour one minute and zooming up to ninety the next. We have tried, unsuccessfully, to ground him: hiding his keys, calling up his ophthalmologist and asking him to order Poppy not to drive, removing the distributor cap, but nothing works.

"Dashing through the snow," he begins to sing, "in a one-horse open sleigh . . ."

He trails off, disappointed that we haven't jollily joined him, but Cease is hung over and I'm not in the mood.

"What a bunch of party poopers," Poppy says. "Where's your Christmas spirit?"

"Bah, humbug," Cease says.

"Gingerly," Poppy says, ignoring Cease, "have you bought your mother's present from me yet?"

"No," I tell him, "I haven't had a chance to go downtown. I was thinking I'd get her a new bathrobe, something in a heavy silk, like a man's smoking jacket."

"I want you to get her that typewriter she wants," he says. "One that doesn't beep."

I'm surprised. The first time Virginia mentioned wanting the typewriter, two or three years ago, he said, "What for? What have you got to say?" and the subject was dropped. I always figured he was afraid, afraid of their both retreating to their respective typewriters after dinner, afraid that she might finish before he did, afraid, as well, of what she might say about him, afraid he might be faced with the reality of her.

"*I* could write a book," Cease says, and Poppy says sure he could. "They say everybody has one book in him."

"Who's 'they'?" I ask.

"Huh?" Poppy asks.

"Who's 'they'?" I repeat. "*Who* says everybody has one book in him? Or her?"

"'Or *her,*'" Cease mutters. "My sister, the feminazi."

"It's a figure of speech," Poppy says. "You ought to know that, Gingervitis, you're the professor around here."

"What I want to know is who 'they' are," I say, and he tells me to stop being a schoolmarm, it doesn't matter who "they" is.

"But it does matter," I say. "You can't go around quoting some vague 'they' as if 'they' spoke the truth."

"'They' is common knowledge," Poppy says. "It's shorthand for something somebody once said, something that's common knowledge now. That's who 'they' is."

"But who is that somebody? Who said it in the first place?"

"Who cares?" Cease says. "Who cares except you and a few other obsessive-compulsive techno twits?"

I restrain myself from reaching forward and smashing Cease's head into the glove compartment.

"'They' can say anything," I continue. "'They' can say, 'Russians eat babies for breakfast' and quote some made-up statistic and before you know it, half the country is going around saying, 'Well, you know, they say Russians eat babies for breakfast.'"

"Don't they?" Cease asks and Poppy laughs so hard he swerves the car onto the shoulder.

"Poppy!" I cry. "Watch out!"

"What?" he says, swerving the car back into the middle of the road. "What?"

I suppose dying in a car wreck with Poppy and Cease is as good a way as any to go. I don't have a great fear of death— I'm not looking forward to it and I have a great deal of work

I'd like to get done before I go, and I would, if possible, like to enjoy life a little before I let go of it, if for no other reason than to discover why it is most people cling to it so tenaciously. The only thing I ask of death is that it be painless and quick, and, since I'm not asking for anything else—long life or great riches or fame—I like to think death will grant me that.

"Here we are!" Poppy announces as he pulls into the Abbots' driveway. It's only 5:00 A.M., there is no sign of life out at the garage, but the lights are on in the house and Floyd opens the back door to peer out at us as we drive slowly up.

Poppy honks the horn and I cringe, thinking of poor Mrs. Abbot up in her bed, trying to get a few hours respite from her arthritis.

"Poppy!" I scold, "it's five o'clock in the morning!"

"What?" he asks defensively. "Floyd's up."

He pushes a button and Cease's window lowers.

"Floyd!" Poppy shouts. "Are we too early?"

Of course we're too early. Poppy knows damn well we're too early but he also knows Floyd Abbot will indulge him, as everybody does. Poppy may be infuriating and thoughtless but he's also kind and generous, and a month from now he'll be sitting at the dinner table, eating one of those mail-order steaks he adores and he'll pause and say to Virginia, "You know, I wonder if we woke Harriet up." Virginia won't bother to ask what he means, he could be talking about something he did the day before or a decade before. "I wonder how she's getting on," he'll say. "Think I'll send them some steaks," and a few days later Floyd and Harriet will receive two boxes of mail-order steaks, and Harriet, I'd be willing to bet, will know exactly why.

"How you doing, Cecil?" Floyd asks, pulling a fur-hooded parka around his lean farmer's body and approaching the car. "I've got a great tree for you. Been saving it. Half the folks comin' out here wanted it, but I told 'em no, that one's for Cecil Moore."

It's true. He'll take us out to a big, beautiful tree, fat and green, but Poppy will want to pick out his own. He'll find some scrawny, diseased tree Floyd couldn't get rid of, and point to it and say, "How about that one?" and Floyd will be embarrassed, he wants us to have a good tree, but Poppy likes them "lean," the others have too many needles. He'll pick the scraggliest one available and by the time we get it home it will be half-naked and Virginia will come downstairs and say, "Oh, I see you've put up the Fire Hazard," and everybody will laugh.

Floyd folds himself into the backseat with me and we drive out to the barn to pick up the axe and the chain saw.

Poppy wants to know how business is and Floyd shakes his head and says he thinks people are going back to fake trees again. For a while there, all this eco stuff was great for business, everybody wanted natural, and not just natural but straight from the earth, but business hasn't been too good this year.

"This eco stuff," he says sadly. "It's just like everything else nowadays. The kooks get involved and take it too far and regular people just don't know what's right; it's right to have natural but it's wrong to cut down a tree and they don't realize that these trees are planted to *be* cut down, that's what they're there for." He sighs. "Bunch of sheep," he says. "Don't even know their own minds, waiting for somebody else to tell 'em what they're supposed to do this year."

Poppy laughs. "Well, you can count on us, Floyd," and Floyd says he knows that, he always says, now Cecil Moore, there's a man knows his own mind, there's a man you can rely on.

We pick up Floyd's things from the barn and drive down a rutty road between dark rows of Douglas fir. I have always preferred Scotch pine; they seem softer and fuller than the firs, more elegant, but Floyd grows firs and Floyd was Poppy's client and what's fair is fair, Poppy always says.

We reach the end of a row and Floyd tells Poppy to stop. We all climb out of the car and Cease and I lean against it, shivering, while Poppy and Floyd argue about the tree. Poppy wins, as always. Cease's and my job is to be the cheering squad, to clap with delight as Poppy makes the first cut, to run squealing for cover when Floyd starts up the chain saw and brings the tree down. This is the point, every year, when I vow never to come back for Christmas, to come instead at some nontraditional time, when I can at least make the pretense of being an adult, where every minute isn't scripted, down to our facial expressions.

"Tally ho!" Floyd says as he hands Poppy the axe, and we laugh on cue as Poppy makes his feeble swing, barely nicking the bark, and Floyd starts his chain saw and we all back away.

It's still pitch-dark by the time Floyd has finished cutting down the tree and tying it in the trunk and having his annual argument with Poppy about paying: Poppy wants to pay and Floyd won't hear of it and what's the difference, he knows he'll get a box or two of steaks out of the deal, and possibly a case of grapefruit if Poppy hears that Harriet is down with the flu.

If we hurry, I think as we drop Floyd off at his house, we can get home, get the tree set up and I can get in a couple hours sleep before it's time to assemble in the den to greet Virginia for her "surprise."

"What are you hiding?" Michael once asked. "Every other woman I've gone out with was dying to take me home to meet her family."

"And you didn't go," I said.

"Hell, no," he said. "That's the last step before the fucking altar; you meet a woman's parents and you might as well slip on the ball and chain then and there."

"Then why do you want to meet my parents?" I asked. "Is this your perverse way of asking me to marry you?"

He turned a kind of seasick green and began to sputter. I was just playing with him, but he didn't know that. I'm not exactly the femme fatale type; I have no patience for plots, and frankly, even if I did, I'm not the kind of woman who can pull it off. There is nothing mysterious about me, nothing dangerous, nothing that a man could hook an obsession on, nothing that could make him lie awake for weeks, wondering what I was up to. No man would ever ruin his life for me, and it's just as well, I couldn't handle the responsibility.

"You're like someone with a fatal illness," Cassie always says. "You give everything away as if you'll never need it again."

"What's to save?" I asked, and she said that wasn't the point, the point was to have fun, to play with your food before you ate it, but I guess I'm just not the playful type.

"Uh, well, gee, uh, you know I love you, Ginger," Michael said, but I didn't know any such thing. What Michael and I sometimes have is more than friendship, more than lust, more than what people call a "casual affair," but it's less than love. It can pass for love, and sometimes, in my more rapturous moments, I can make myself believe it is love. It's similar to what I've always had that passed for love, but it isn't what I imagine love to be.

As Virginia says, I have no idea what love is. Cassie and I are forever having debates about romantic love: she doesn't believe in it and yet she's always in love; I believe in it with a kind of schoolgirl passion and yet I'm never in love. Love, for me, has always been so painful that I couldn't imagine why anyone would want it. The only person in my life it was a pleasure to love, besides Fritz, was India, and now even that is tainted.

I wonder if Poppy knows about India. He might; he was in Paris during the war, and Poppy being Poppy, he would certainly have looked up the mother of his bride-to-be. But he's never mentioned it and since he's told us about every second he spent overseas I suppose he didn't see her there. It's odd. Odd that he didn't see her, odd that he's never mentioned it, odd that no one has ever asked, "Did you ever see India when you were in Paris?"

I suppose I should discuss it with him, especially before I go to the trouble of driving all over town looking for a beep-less typewriter, but I won't. It doesn't matter if he knows, it doesn't matter, ultimately, if Virginia finds out. I can't protect her from the truth; it's there, it exists, and while I don't have to flaunt it in her face, I don't have to hide it from her, either.

9

"YOU ARE SO CONTROLLING," MICHAEL ALWAYS SAYS, AND he's right. I *am* controlling. It's another reason I prefer the dead to the living; the dead will let me climb inside, the living won't. Not that I blame them—I wouldn't want anyone snooping around inside of me, either, and in fact that's why I stopped analysis. I always imagined Greta in a plaid cap and trenchcoat, poking and prying and wandering around inside my head with her magnifying glass, trying to root out clues I didn't want her to find.

Not that I have anything to hide—it's just the idea of it I didn't like. It was a little too Orwellian for me; I was afraid she'd find my greatest fear and then attack me with it, put it in a cage and attach it to my head and let the starving rats of my unconscious eat my face off.

I wouldn't last a second under torture. In fact, the idea of torture *is* my greatest fear; I worry about it the way some people worry about getting cancer or being in a plane crash. I worry I'll be falsely accused of a horrible crime I didn't commit in some fascistic country where I've never been and they'll kidnap me and toss me in a putrid cell and threaten me with torture if I don't confess and so I'll confess and they'll torture me anyway. I never imagine what the torture is, the mere idea of any kind of torture is enough to get me rolled up under the bed.

I have no idea where that comes from. I suppose the seeds were sown along with the conspiracy seeds back in the McCarthy era, when the country was seething with paranoia. I often wonder why those, the dark seeds, took root, while the others, the happy peaceful benign little seedlets of contentment that everyone else seems to have nurtured during the fifties never so much as formed a bud in me.

I am, frankly, a coward. "You're afraid of everything but stiffs," Michael has said, but I'm afraid of them, too. When one works with ghosts, as I do, one begins to believe in them, not in pale white puffs drifting through locked doors, or lumbering, malignant spectres draped in chains and brandishing the weapon with which they were murdered, but rather in the force of their energy. When I'm working on a book it's as if I'm taken over by my subject, as if I become Sarah Fielding or Angeline Wilton or, now, Charlotte Cibber. I never realize it's happening; in fact, I am always struck by how remarkably alike we are, down to the slight lisp we develop under stress, or the annoying habit we have of speaking of ourselves in the third person, as if we weren't there. It's only when I finish, when I send my subject back to the grave and return myself to the living, that I realize I have never had a lisp and I have certainly never referred to myself as "Ginger."

When I was working on Angeline I would go into deep

depressions in which I would lie on the lumpy little couch in my bed-sit and "remember" walking through the gardens of Blethen House, Angeline's father's country place, with Charles, the man who "disappointed" Angeline. I was quite shocked, when I was revising my manuscript, to find several references to rather steamy sexual escapades between Angeline and Charles, which I had to delete, of course, having no proof of their existence other than my having relived them in my bed-sit.

As I mentioned before, I am not a particularly imaginative person, so I attribute these fantasies to the ghosts of my subjects. How else would I have known about the little thatched cottage behind the rose garden where Angeline and Charles used to screw? I had never been to Blethen House, at least not at that point, and when I did go, after Christmas, when Poppy and Virginia sent me a check and I could finally afford the price of a return ticket, I wasn't the least surprised to find it—a ruin now, with just a few ivy-covered stones remaining, but exactly where I knew it would be.

I suppose I could have read about it somewhere else, in her father's journals or her brother's diary or in someone's letters, but I prefer to think Angeline herself visited me, that she wanted me to know everything about her, that she wanted me to know she wasn't the prudish, bitter old maid she appeared to be.

I'm not afraid of visits from the ghosts of my subjects, nor even of losing my own identity for a while, having it usurped by their spirits. What I am afraid of is displeasing them, of having them come back and haunt me for not leaving out the part about beating the servant girls.

The light is on in Virginia's room, but Poppy pretends not to notice and it goes off as soon as we pull in the driveway.

"Shhhhh," he hisses as Cease slams his door. "Don't wake your mother."

"An AK-47 couldn't wake her up," Cease says, and I think how odd it is that the AK-47 has replaced the "ten-ton bomb" of our youth. We no longer fear the anonymous annihilation of an "enemy bomb," we fear instead a personal attack with a gun wielded by an individual, most likely black and crack-crazed, who decides to drive seventy-five miles from the nearest inner city to threaten our middle-class peacefulness. Michael could do something with that, and if I decide to call him back, I'll tell him. Merry Christmas, dear, here's an idea for you.

He hates that. "Everybody thinks they're a comic," he complains. "I can't walk down the street without somebody giving me a fucking *idea*. If they're so funny, why don't *they* get up on stage?" But the reason they give him the idea is *because* they can't get up on stage, and I tell him that. "If they could get up and do it themselves, they certainly wouldn't be handing out their ideas to the competition," I tell him, but it still drives him nuts.

Poppy and Cease untie the tree and drag it in the house while I set up the stand and bring the boxes of decorations up from the basement. I can't help it, I get sappy and sentimental when I unpack the decorations—two of each, one for Cease and one for me, to place on the tree when we were small, and to keep for our own tree when we grew up. It never occurred to anyone that we would never grow up, that we would still be coming back here for Christmas decades after we should have had homes of our own, homes with lots of grandchildren for Poppy to delight and Virginia to terrorize.

All we ever wanted to do, we told each other, was to get the hell out of here and here we are. We are "out of here" in the sense that we don't live in this house anymore, that we live, in fact, far from North Bay, on opposite coasts of the country, but "here" is a place from which we will never escape, no matter how far we go or how old we become. We are stuck, forever, trapped in the moment when Virginia disappeared, waiting hopelessly for her to return.

It's humiliating. Cease and I are both, at forty-one and thirty-eight years of age, respectively, approaching middle age, but despite the years and the hard knocks (two years in Vietnam for Cease, a broken marriage apiece, several muggings and three spirit-destroying years in the New York City Social Services Department for me) we are still like sad little waifs, crying in the night for Mommy.

At least I know what's going on, although the knowledge doesn't help much. I'll probably be coming back here until I'm eighty, until we're all senile and useless, sitting around the kitchen table in our diapers and bibs, with Poppy still making up goofball names for us and Cease still playing "Dysfunctional Families."

"Let it go," I tell him every year, but he can't. Hating Virginia is his *raison d'être,* and God only knows what he'd be if he didn't have her to hate. He is my brother, and I love him, but the truth is, he does have a number of the characteristics of a serial killer. Whenever I read about some new psychopath roaming around the West Coast, I have to call him, to make sure he hasn't gone over the edge. He wouldn't, of course, he's sick but harmless, at least as far as anyone other than Virginia is concerned. The method in his madness is simple: get Virginia. And get her not in the sense of physically hurting her, just constantly pricking at her with her own inadequacies, torturing her with her own fears, sending her clippings, for example, on "Shaken Baby Syndrome."

He says he's in therapy but I doubt it. He's got the babble down, but anyone with a TV set can manage the basic vocabulary. There's nothing in his behavior to indicate he's made even the slightest attempt to understand either himself or anyone else. "I hate the world and everyone in it," he always says, and Virginia says, "Well, at least no one can accuse me of raising prejudiced children." "You didn't raise me at all," Cease says in return, just another exchange of snappy comebacks at the Moore home.

This year's tree is the most pathetic we've had so far; Poppy and Cease have got it up and leaning drunkenly into the bookcase, its scrawny limbs sticking out like a drying rack, which, at least, makes it easier to hang the decorations. Poppy opens the cabinet under the stereo and begins searching for the scratchy old album of Anita Bryant singing Christmas carols, which he'll play over my objection, singing *sotto voce* until Virginia arrives, at which point he'll pump up the volume and we'll all be expected to join in.

Actually, the carols are a boon; as long as Cease and Poppy are intent on the Three Kings of Orient Are we don't have to talk, and the closer we get to Christmas the more dangerous talking becomes. Memories will start popping up, happy ones for Poppy, darker ones for the rest of us, and the holiday will deteriorate into a free-for-all, with Cease attacking Virginia, Virginia attacking herself, Poppy retreating to his study—which leaves me, always the good little charwoman, to pick up the pieces.

"Why do you go?" Cassie asks every year and every year I give her the same answer, a shrug; I suppose I keep hoping that every year will be the one in which we give up the drama, put away the grudges, and just enjoy each other despite our many flaws. And they are, after all, my family, the only family I've got, and as infuriating and downright vile as they can sometimes be, I do love them. Besides, in my work, I've come across families that make mine look like that fantasy family all middle-class Americans are supposed to have. Cease's spiteful sadism and Virginia's drunkenness and Poppy's oblivion seem almost sweet and homely in comparison.

For instance, one Christmas, Angeline's father, always the

joker, gave her a box full of horseshit as a present. She'd been begging for a horse of her own—in addition to the carriage horses and work horses, he had a whole stable full of valuable horses he kept as status symbols, to show off to his horsey guests. He didn't ride them or race them or do anything at all with them, he just *had* them, along with a crew of grooms who did nothing but brush them and let them out to run and keep them looking beautiful for the guests to gape at. So Angeline, ever the optimist, thought the box of horseshit went along with a colt and she ran out to the stable, where, in a stall decorated with Christmas bunting and with a note that said "FOR ANGELINE," she found her gift: a colt, yes, but a dead one.

Not even Cease could be that cruel, although he's come close. One year he talked about giving Virginia a doll he'd made that turned blue if you shook it and I spent the whole morning shuddering every time Virginia reached for a box with her name on it. Fortunately, he was just bullshitting. He gave her a decanter that played "How Dry I Am" every time you took out the stopper, cruel enough, but a relief compared to the doll.

"What a waste," Virginia always says about Cease, and it's true. One year, when I was having noise trouble with my upstairs neighbor, he made me a little gizmo to attach to my ceiling that shouted "Shut up or I'll have my dog tear you to pieces!" in a gruff, mobster-like voice, complete with vicious dog sounds in the background. It went off automatically whenever the noise reached a certain decibel level, but I was afraid to use it, afraid the guy in 6D would come down and tear *me* to pieces, so I gave it to Michael, and he uses it all the time.

"Silver bells," Poppy sings, "silver bells . . ."

He stops when he hears Virginia coughing on the stairs, stumbling her way down for her surprise.

"Another year, another chance to burn down the house," she says as she surveys the tree and Poppy giggles and gives her a hug.

"Just like old times," he says, and Cease, for once, doesn't say a thing, he just grins and hangs another clump of tinsel on a drooping branch.

10

ANGELINE WILTON, AFTER VIEWING HER DEAD COLT, DID something that endeared her to me forever. She left her father and brother in the barn, wiping tears of laughter from their eyes, and marched back to the house, took the box of horseshit, went to her father's bedroom, and stuffed his pillow full of manure. He was too drunk when he went to bed, and too hung over in the morning, to notice, but that wasn't the point, the point was to *do* something, to take an action, to stand up for herself, to not run into the woods and hide and cry her little heart out. She was ten years old at the time, and although her father never knew what she had done (the maid, of course, having removed the pillow when she made his bed), Angeline at least had the consolation of knowing that she hadn't crumbled, that she had, however feebly, struck back.

She spent most of the rest of her life planning her little retaliations, a terrible waste of energy, especially since they were always secret. No one knew she had emptied her chamber pot into her father's wine barrel or that she had sawed through the leg of the guest of honor's chair so he would crash inelegantly on his bum during dinner. She was always so dismayed when these catastrophes occurred, so horrified, that the suspicion never settled on her. She wrote about them boldly and proudly, in her diary, noting with malicious glee the look of panic and fear spreading over her father's face when some insignificant member of the royal family found little brown deer pellets in her salad, knowing that her father didn't find her interesting enough to snoop through her drawers. What could she, a silly girl, have to say?

The very words Poppy used to Virginia. Well, not the silly girl part. Poppy, unlike Cease, isn't intentionally brutal, he's just oblivious. His cruelty lacks malice, it's the cruelty of a child asking why you stink, he doesn't mean to hurt your feelings, he just wants to know.

Cease, on the other hand, puts a great deal of thought into his attacks. I imagine him sitting in his trailer out in the Oregon woods, tinkering with his toys and dreaming up ways to torment Virginia. As far as I know, that's all he does; he doesn't have a job and he certainly doesn't have a girlfriend. No buddies, except, of course, *Norm*. None of us are sure how he gets by and we're afraid to ask, although that really doesn't make much sense. If he were doing something horrible, like selling drugs or working for the Mafia or making pornographic videos or getting welfare, he'd be sure to flaunt it in Virginia's face.

"Ahhhh," Virginia sighs, walking over to the tree and adjusting one of the papier-mâché hummingbirds, "Aunt Asia's birds."

"Get ready for a trip down Memory Lane," Cease says and Virginia glares at him.

"I wasn't going to tell the story," she says and Cease says, "Good. Because we've already heard it five million times. I can tell it backwards. 'Present Christmas a me send to bothered even hadn't she that furious was Asia and left had Mother after year the was it.'"

We all stare at him and I wonder how much time he wasted memorizing that long and convoluted story backwards.

"That's not backwards," Virginia says, "that's only the first sentence backwards."

"Okay," Cease says, " 'these me made Asia so and . . .'"

"What do you say we go to Quinlan's for breakfast?" Poppy asks. Going out to eat is his solution to every problem and, generally, it works. It at least changes the subject.

"I don't like Quinlan's," Virginia says. "You can't smoke there anymore."

"What difference does that make?" Poppy asks. "You don't smoke when you eat, anyway."

"I smoke *before* I eat. I smoke *after* I eat."

"Well, you can go out to the car and smoke," Poppy suggests, but no, Virginia isn't going to sit in the car like some juvenile delinquent just because Theresa Quinlan is an anti-smoker. "She's just too good to be true," Virginia mutters and I suggest that Cease and Poppy go to Quinlan's and Virginia and I can go down to St. Clair and have brunch at the Inn and do some Christmas shopping.

"Doesn't that sound like a good idea?" I ask.

"I loathe Christmas shopping," Virginia says and I tell her we can skip the shopping, then, and just have brunch. "Champagne brunch," I say and she perks up.

"Do they have screwdrivers?" she asks and I say I'm sure

they do. I wonder how long it's been since she's been out; she acts as if she's never been to brunch, and quite possibly, she hasn't.

"Sounds like a plan," Poppy says. "The girls and the boys." Cease rolls his eyes, he doesn't care where he goes, or with whom, as long as the food is plentiful and free.

"C'mon, Cease," Poppy says, throwing a fatherly arm around his shoulder, "steak and eggs. Man food," and they leave, crunching the shedded tree needles as they go.

"We don't have to go out," I tell Virginia as soon as they leave. "I just suggested that to get rid of them."

"I used to love Christmas," Virginia says as she walks into the kitchen, heading straight for the liquor cupboard. "Now I hate it." She grabs a bottle of vodka and waves it at me. "Always plenty of screwdrivers at Chez Moore," she says.

"Why is that?" I ask. "I mean, why do you hate Christmas?"

"Why do you think?" she snarls. "Because everybody is supposed to be happy all the time, happy, happy, happy, it makes me sick."

She downs her drink and fixes another. "It's such a stupid word. 'Happy.' It doesn't sound joyous; it sounds like a slap. I hate it. It's stupid."

I can see it's going to be another fun-filled day at Chez Moore and I suddenly wish I hadn't given up smoking, that I too could do something to self-destruct. Christmas fills us all with self-pity, but it's worst for Virginia, since it was supposedly her job to create the happy family we all so grievously mourn, her only job and she fucked it up. "You think it's all my fault," she says every year, and it's true, we do, even Poppy, on the rare occasions when he'll admit we're not the perfect little American microcosm, for it must be someone's fault and who else's could it be? He did *his* job. He brought home the bacon and mowed the lawn and played catch with

Cease and took us to the Dairy Queen and made up jokes—what more could anyone ask?

"Haaappp-pee," Virginia says, drawing it out obscenely. "It was one of your grandmother's favorite words. She always ended her letters with 'Be Happy,' as if that were possible living in that moldy old mausoleum with Asia and Florida, two women who never uttered that word in their lives. If she wanted me to be haaappp-pee, why didn't she send for me?"

There was a war going on, but that was no excuse as far as Virginia was concerned, Nazis were nothing compared to that pair of life-hating hags; in fact they should have been Nazis, they probably *were* Nazis, they certainly loved discipline and hated "nigras" enough to be Nazis.

She waves the bottle at me again. "Want one?" she asks and I say, "Yuk. It's seven o'clock in the morning."

"Good. I never drink before five," she says and laughs gaily, as if it's all just one long and very funny joke.

"They hated her, you know," she says, bringing her drink over to the table and sitting down. "They were jealous. All that life she had. Full of it, Mother was, and they had nothing but a bunch of Confederate geezers buried in the backyard."

She reaches in her pocket and pulls out a bent cigarette.

"They tried to make me hate her, too," she says as she lights the cigarette. "And of course I did hate her for leaving me with them. But I didn't hate *her*. Like you hate me."

"I don't hate you, Virginia," I say, wearily.

"How could I hate her?" she asks. "She was a war hero. A member of the Resistance. At least she left me to do something good in the world, something important, something fine and brave. She didn't give me much, but at least she gave me that."

I nod, feeling sick at heart, wondering what she will do when she discovers the truth about India, when she finds out the only thing she ever gave her was a lie? Being abandoned by a hero is one thing, but being abandoned by a collaborator is another entirely.

"Maybe the Geography Aunts had a reason to hate her," I suggest, tentatively, and Virginia harrumphs.

"Of course they had a reason," she says. "She was alive and they were dead. The dead always hate the living."

"You should know," Cease would say if he were here, and I feel guilty and vile for allowing myself to play his part, if only in my head.

"Did they always hate her?" I ask.

"How should I know?" Virginia says. "Mother was never around to tell me about her childhood, and all Florida and Asia ever talked about was Uncle Beauregard and his plantation. The Willows. The Willows, The Willows, The Willows, as if it had been something straight out of *Gone with the Wind,* as if they'd lost something of value, as if they could have been anything other than dried-up old crows if the South hadn't lost the war. Do you know what The Willows was?"

Of course I know, but I shake my head.

"A little two-story clapboard house. A nothing. A run-down farm. It was worthless before the war and worthless afterward. But blaming the war—the Civil War, of course, the others didn't matter to them—for all their woes was their favorite pastime."

I wonder if they were really that bad. I could find out. I could go down to Holly Hill and interview people who knew them, I could go down to the Historical Society and look through their papers, for they kept every scrap of paper, every letter, every amateur family history—Florida, in fact, wrote a new, up-dated version sometime back in the fifties— every clipping, every photograph, anything that had to do with Family. Florida offered it all to Virginia, the last of the Curries, but she didn't want it. "Who wants an attic full of

lies and bad memories?" she said and hung up and that was
the last she heard from the Geography Aunts.

I am not particularly interested in my own history, especially the southern side of it. I am much too cowardly to unearth those skeletons. I don't really want to know how many
slaves my great-great-grandparents owned and I certainly
don't want to know how they treated them. As a child, however, I couldn't get enough of the Geography Aunts and
Uncle Beauregard and Miss Dawson's Academy, where Virginia went to learn to be a Lady. And of course I was en-
thralled by Granny, heroic Granny, hiding out in the French
countryside sabotaging Nazi supply lines, or whatever she
did. What Virginia lacked in clarity she made up for in feats
of heroism, to the point where I grew up believing that my
grandmother had single-handedly won the war.

Virginia didn't make it up from whole cloth, of course, she
just embellished what India told her, in her infrequent letters,
making her a little bit larger and a little bit braver and a little
more important than she made herself, which was not insub-
stantial to begin with.

"I don't remember ever hearing laughter in that house,"
Virginia is saying. "I suppose that's why I married your father. He made me laugh."

Oh, God. I wonder if that's why I'm with Michael, because he makes me laugh, because he brings laughter into an
otherwise joyless life. Not that my life is joyless, I *like* my life,
I adore my friends, my work gives me a great deal of pleasure
and satisfaction, I love New York, but I'm so enveloped in
Virginia's gloom right now that I can't remember what my
own life is like, it seems so distant, almost unreal, as if it were
just something I made up. I feel rather pathetic, as if I were so
identified with Virginia that I had to choose my lover for the
same reasons she chose hers, and I think perhaps I should

break up with Michael, if we're not broken up already. I loathe the idea of clinging to him because I can't make my own laughter, because I am searching for a father replacement, because I am so resourceless.

I want to ask Virginia if she loves Poppy but I can't. I say I want to know who my parents are but the truth is, I'm afraid to find out, there is no way I can find out who they are without having to feel their pain and I'm just not brave enough for that.

So how can I tell her about India? It was bad enough, finding out myself, by mistake, but the shock and disappointment I went through upon discovering that Granny was a fake was nothing compared to what Virginia would feel. To me, it was a jolt, painful but bearable, but to Virginia it would be a disaster, an earthquake that would shatter her whole world and take away the only little bit of pride she has left.

I look at her, sitting across the table with her cigarette dangling from her wrinkled lips, her drink in her hand. She's clutching it as if it were her last link to the world, and I know I will never be the one to tell her. If she finds out on her own, fine, but I will not be the person to tell her that her beloved, heroic mother doesn't exist, that she is, in fact, merely a footnote, a snide remark in someone else's life, that she appears in history only as "The Cow."

11

IN MY WORK I AM ALWAYS DISCOVERING THINGS I DON'T want to know. Bits of information that throw doubt upon, or completely destroy, my theories—a letter here, a journal there, a newspaper item, little lights that shine upon my subject and reveal that what I thought was a lovely birthmark is actually an ugly wart. With the living, there is always the temptation to ignore the truth, blot it out, brush it away, rationalize it, hope that it is only a fluke, a passing phase, that this too, as they say, shall pass. One can, of course, do the same with the dead, and in fact most of us do. We like to remember those we love, those we admire or emulate, in their most flattering guise, conveniently forgetting, or ignoring, the uglier aspects of their characters, the petty flaws that would tarnish an otherwise perfect memory.

Frankly, I'm rather fond of flaws, so long as they don't undermine my thesis. They add depth to characters, humanize them, give them what Cassie calls a "rooting interest."

India's flaws are another matter. It would be one thing if she had been merely a fraud. Frauds can be quite endearing; I always feel a great deal of tenderness toward people who try to make their lives grander than they are, especially those who go to great lengths to do so. In a way, that in itself is rather grand, shedding the old life and, in lieu of having a new one that is in itself notable, making it up.

I make a distinction between frauds and phonies: phonies aren't the least bit interesting to me, they're shallow and lazy, changing on a whim, to make an impression or strike a pose, to climb their ladder of choice, be it social or economic or artistic or whatever—they're all affect, remaining at the core the same person, generally a rather dull one, whereas the fraud *becomes* the character he has created for himself, he lives the life he has made up, he even, in many cases, grows to believe it himself. Frauds are, to me, a sort of benign sociopath; phonies are just assholes.

India, I'm afraid, was both. I found out about her several years ago, when I was thinking about writing Nancy Cunard's life. Nancy appealed to me in many ways: she was bold and wild and headstrong and artistic and determined to carve out a spot for herself in the world. But I wasn't really comfortable with her aristocratic background. Nancy herself professed to despise it, but the fact remained that she had it and I would have to deal with it. I prefer to work within my own milieu, not because I am a great supporter of middle-class values, whatever they may be, but rather because the world of the bourgeoisie is one I understand. Nancy's world, the world of privilege and wealth and power, is a world I am familiar with only from books. The concept of entitlement is completely alien to me; I feel I must *earn* everything, including the right to breathe, every single day. There is no resting on one's laurels, as wilted and puny as they may be, and I awake every morning thinking I must earn my right to be on the planet. I go to bed every night choking on guilt for not having done so.

Be that as it may, I felt that in order to do justice to Nancy, I would have had to have a greater understanding of her world and that was a leap I knew I couldn't make at the time.

As it turned out, I didn't even try. I had immersed myself in Nancy's world, reading all about Paris in the thirties and forties, and I began to wonder why none of the people India had supposedly known—not Sylvia Beach, Janet Flanner, Ernest Hemingway, none of the emigré Americans—had mentioned her in their letters or diaries or autobiographies. I knew she was never a major player—the columns she had sent back to the *Holly Hill Gazette* weren't exactly Pulitzer Prize material; they were mostly about how the Nazis were raining on her parade and how impossible it was to get a decent pair of gloves, but that, supposedly, was her "cover," she was posing as a rather silly southern belle so the Nazis would never suspect her of being a saboteur.

I finally found her. A footnote in Drue Tartiere's diary of the Occupation. "The Cow was here today, sniffing about and eating all the food. I told P I thought she was too stupid to be a spy. P said, 'The stupid ones are the most dangerous.'" The footnote read: "'The Cow' was Tartiere's code name for India Lee Currie, an American journalist suspected of collaboration."

I didn't believe it. I couldn't believe it. And I was furious with Drue for referring to my grandmother as stupid. "The Cow" I could understand—Granny was rather large and awkward, and no one's food was safe when she was around, but stupid she wasn't. I should have dropped the matter there, but I didn't. The footnote said "suspected of" and I decided I would vindicate her, that I would prove that she had indeed been a hero, that, in fact, her silly southern belle cover had been so effective it had fooled even the Underground.

I couldn't bear the idea of India spending the rest of eternity as "The Cow," so I began to dig. It was hard work and, ultimately, futile. I found a few more references to "The Cow" and a few to India herself, always in the context of being a hanger-on, an uninvited guest, eager and needy, which even in the best of times is enough to make one suspect; in dark times, one is suspected of the worst. It was impossible, from the little information available, to discover whether or not India was a traitor—everyone in France claimed to have been a member of the Resistance; everyone they didn't like was suspected of being a collaborator—but I knew in my heart she wasn't. India wasn't interested in money or power or vengeance, the things the Nazis could have offered her in exchange for what droppings of information she could have swept up off the floor. She wanted only to be liked, and to be liked by the people she admired, worshipped, emulated, the people she wanted to be but wasn't. She definitely wasn't a hero, she was just a frightened, fat, lonely woman who wanted to be better than she thought she was.

So, to us, back home, she was a fraud—she truly was what she made herself out to be: glamorous, exotic, courageous, larger than life. It never occurred to us to doubt her, and why should we, we loved what she was, we believed her because it suited us as much as it suited her. To the people in Paris who she claimed were her friends, she was a phony, a mere irritant, a nothing they'd brush off with a contemptuous remark.

It was all too sad. When I found out about India, I gave up on Nancy Cunard and in fact closed the book, so to speak, on that entire period of history, at least as far as subject matter was concerned.

"I went to see her once, you know," Virginia says. "Did I ever tell you that?"

I'm shocked. I didn't think there was one instant of Virginia's life she hadn't inflicted upon us. Virginia isn't one for telling shaggy-dog stories, that's Poppy's domain, but I'm suspicious. How could it be that a woman who had pummeled us with every event in her rather eventless life would hold back something as important as a trip to Paris to seek out her mother?

"No," I say, "when was that?"

"1948. I was still in college at the time. I sold my engagement ring to book passage."

"You sold your engagement ring? What did Poppy say?"

Virginia laughs. "Nothing. He never knew." She holds her hand out and waves the large diamond in my face.

"It's glass," she says. "He never knew the difference." She struggles to pull it off her finger, but it's stuck. "I've left it to you in my will. I hope you're not planning to make a down payment on a house with it."

I hadn't been planning to do anything with it; I hadn't known she was leaving it to me, but at least it's good to know it's worthless so I can save myself the humiliation of trying to sell it at some pawn shop if I get desperate.

"Well?" I ask.

"Well, what?"

"Well, what happened?"

"She took me shopping," Virginia says.

"That's it?"

She shrugs and heaves herself up from the table.

"That's it," she says. "She bought me a trousseau. Lace nighties and things like that."

"But didn't you talk to her? Didn't you meet any of her friends? Didn't you go anywhere? The Louvre? The playground in the Tuileries she was always talking about?"

"We went shopping. We went out to eat. We shopped and we ate, shopped and ate, ate and shopped. Of course we didn't talk, our mouths were always full."

She's lying, of course. One doesn't sell one's engagement ring and sail across the ocean just to shop, at least not people like us.

"I had an affair," she says. She leans against the counter and runs her hand through her hair, pulling it back off her face and revealing the deep straight lines across her forehead, like scars, and I am amazed I had never noticed them before. She's old. Much, much older than I had thought.

"With an Italian. A real Latin lover. I was a virgin, of course, but I thought since I was in Paris I might as well learn about love. Get some experience to take back with my nighties."

She walks over to the cupboard and takes out a cup and saucer, the good, not the everyday.

"I met this man and he seemed utterly charming," she says as she pours herself a cup of coffee. "Very aristocratic. Very tall-dark-and-handsome. Mysterious. European. Sexy, I suppose, although I had no idea what sex was."

She laughs again, a hard, flat, mirthless laugh.

"I was quite beautiful then, young and lovely and fresh, and I really could have had my pick of men. I'm not saying this to brag, it's just true, I had that pale, starved look that was so fashionable then, as if I had suffered a great deal. Apparently, that was very sexy."

She sighs. "I went to his hotel room with him and we drank champagne and we had sex, I can't call it making love because it was rather awful, I bled all over everything and he was furious, he kept screaming at me in Italian and finally I just pulled on my clothes and fled. When I got back to Mother's rooms, she took one look at me and said, 'Well, I hope it was worth it!' and disappeared into her bedroom. She never said another word about it, she just packed me up and sent me off, back home. To your father. I was terrified he'd know, he'd find out what I'd done and leave me, but I should have known better, he didn't notice a thing, our honeymoon was over in about twenty minutes, and it's been pretty much the same ever since."

I don't want to hear this. I feel vaguely ashamed of myself, for not being mature enough and sophisticated enough to accept my mother's sexuality, but I can't help it, it seems creepy to me. I don't want to think about her rolling around on a bloody bed with a screaming Italian, I don't want to think about her having sex at all.

"Virginia," I say, "I don't think this is appropriate," and she glares at me. "I just don't think this is the kind of thing you should discuss with your daughter. It's the kind of thing you should discuss with your friends."

"I don't *have* any friends," she screams, grabbing the first thing at hand, a spoon lying on the counter, and hurling it at me. "I don't have *anything*!" she shouts and I jump from the chair and flee, running up the stairs while her voice chases after me. "That's right," it shrieks. "Desert me, abandon me in my hour of need . . ." and I slam my door shut and jump into bed, covering my head with my pillow.

12

I AM DROWNING, I AM BEING BURIED ALIVE.

"You're mixing your metaphors," Greta says. "Which is it? Drowning or buried alive?"

I wake up before I can strangle her, which is a shame. If I'd killed her, if only in a dream, I would have spent the morning worrying about my unconscious murderous impulses. Instead, I'll have to waste the entire day thinking about suffocating in other people's lives, worrying about allowing my own chance for Life with a capital L to pass by unheeded and unmourned, at least until it was too late, at which point I'd mourn it all the more.

"Live!" Henry James's characters are always telling each other, but what does that *mean*? Apparently, James didn't think either his own life or that of his main characters qualified as "living" but what does? What pushes one over the edge, what does it take to earn the upper case?

"You think too much," Michael said when I asked him that question. "Look at it this way: if you have to ask, you're not doing it."

Normally, secondhand life is good enough for me, not because it's what I want but because it's all I can handle. Sometimes, however, I wake up in the middle of the night in a panic—"I should be *living!*" I think. "I should be a war correspondent!" I'm not quite sure why going overseas to chronicle death and destruction qualifies as "Life," but rationality is not my strong point when I awaken in a panic. It has to do with "doing," and not just doing anything, but doing something Important, for if it's not Important it isn't *doing,* and if it isn't *doing* it isn't Life.

The logical answer is "India." I think I have to be a war correspondent because that was what she supposedly was and she was the only person I knew who seemed to be *doing,* and doing something Important, the only person I knew who seemed to be living in the world where history happened, which is where I assume one must be in order to be Living.

"This is the life," Michael said as we were lying on the beach in St. Croix, and he meant it, he was having a great time, living it up by just lying on a chaise longue, drinking daiquiris, and soaking up the sun. I, on the other hand, was miserable, slathered in gallons of greasy sunblock and covered head to foot in a caftan, bored to tears despite my pile of books, which I had already made my way halfway through. "Let's go snorkeling," I suggested the first day only to discover, to my bewilderment, that Michael didn't even know how to swim. He also didn't dance or sail or like walking on the beach, all the things one was supposed to do in order to enjoy paradise. He was terrified of horses and allergic to seafood but still he was having a ball.

"Jesus, Ginger," he said at one point, "relax, would you? Why do you always have to be *doing* something?"

I don't know, perhaps he's right, perhaps it's some WASP trait, some genetic tic handed down from the Puritans along with their other fun characteristics. One can no longer blame the culture: the work ethic has long since been replaced by the lottery ethic. You think I exaggerate, but I don't. Three years ago, my high school class reunion committee sent around a questionnaire, and one of the questions was "Plans for the future?" Almost half of my graduating high school class answered: "Win the lottery." "Win the lottery and travel." "Win the lottery and spend the rest of my life fishing." "Win the lottery, ha ha." "Win the lottery and dump my husband."

"Did you see what I wrote?" Melanie asked when she called to gossip about the results.

"'I plan to go right on drinking,'" she said. "Wasn't that good? I got it straight from *Postcards from the Edge*. It's the mother's line. Did you see it?"

"The movie or your answer?"

"The movie, dumbie," she said.

I told her I hadn't. "It's great," she said. "I didn't know Debbie Reynolds was a drunk. At least I'm in good company." I could hear her plopping ice cubes into a glass.

"I wish I could go to one of those celebrity rehabs," she said. "It wouldn't be so bad, drying out with the stars. I hate my rehab. The low-rent rehab. Me and the bag ladies."

She chattered on, complaining about her life, especially about "Him," her fifth husband, whose name she had never mentioned, her words beginning to slur into each other as the conversation continued, or rather deteriorated, and I wondered what she would need to feel alive. Obviously none of the things she had tried had worked, not the five husbands nor the children nor the career nor the boozing and the drugs, none of it felt like living to her, and I wondered what would.

When we were young, all we had wanted from life was to laugh. If we weren't laughing, we weren't alive and if our lives weren't particularly funny, well, then we'd get drunk. When we were drunk everything seemed hilarious and who cared if Melanie's father was a religious fanatic or her brother tried to screw her or she was flunking out of algebra? who cared if Virginia showed up at cheerleading tryouts in a raccoon coat, waving her sorority banner and shouting, "Go, Ginger, go!"? We only talked about these things when we were drunk, when they seemed funny, when we could laugh about them. We never spoke of our problems otherwise; we had an inexplicable gangster mentality, we were supposed to be tough, and the lowest, slimiest, most despicable thing one could be was a crybaby, so we kept everything to ourselves, saving our little heartaches up for the next time we could steal some booze and get drunk and make them funny.

It never occurred to either of us that what we were doing was wrong. It wasn't really dangerous, just dangerous enough to make it appealing, and of course we could quit anytime we wanted—who ever heard of a teenage alcoholic? Of course neither of us could envision a time when we would want to quit; we were just precocious, we told each other, living out the life we would lead in any case, just getting an early start. We'd steal a bottle from Virginia's stash and run off to the cemetery, where we'd hide out behind the mausoleum, by the big old weather-beaten monuments North Bay's founding fathers had had built for themselves, and mix ourselves drinks of Coke and whatever booze we'd grabbed and sit there, drinking and laughing. "Head Start for alkies," Melanie called it and we'd roll around on Peter Peterson's grave, while he looked down disapprovingly, and laugh our heads off.

I suppose I should go see her but I dread it. The last time I talked to her she started screaming at me. "You took me to the edge but you wouldn't jump off," she shouted, and frankly, it's true. I was just as drawn to the edge as she was, but the abyss scared me and Melanie is not the only person I've left floundering down there.

The phone rings several times before Virginia answers it in her room.

"Ginger!" she shouts. "It's for you!"

The only place where one can have a private conversation in our house is Virginia's room, but since she's in there, no doubt reliving her own tumble down into the abyss, I go downstairs, hoping Poppy and Cease won't return and sit around while I'm on the phone, making a running commentary on my side of the conversation.

"Was that your mother?" Michael asks when Virginia hangs up. "She sounds like she just ate a bowl full of gravel."

"She drinks half a fifth of vodka a day and smokes three packs of cigarettes. What do you expect her to sound like?"

"A person," Michael says, "not a cement mixer." He giggles and I can hear him searching through the mess on his bed, looking for a pen to write it down.

There is a pause and then he begins to sing. "I just called . . . to say . . . I loooooovvvvvve you . . ." he sings, and now I know Doris has either booted him out or lost her diaphragm.

I never know what to do when this happens; Cassie always tells me to play hard to get but I don't know how to do that. "Make him work for it," she says, "make him appreciate you," but I'm always so surprised that he'd want me at all, even for a weekend, that I always give in without so much as a "Where have you been?" I suppose it might be different if I thought we would ever be a couple, an unmarried couple, for I don't want to get married again, once was enough, thank you very much. I might act differently if I thought we'd move in together, but I know that will never happen, he'll keep coming around until he finally marries Doris, and he'd keep coming around afterwards, if I'd let him, but I won't. I have to draw the line somewhere, and that's where I draw it. No married men.

After he tells me about Hollywood—this one was a prick and that one was stupid and he doesn't understand how so and so can be a sex symbol because he's ugly as a wart with skin like the FDR Drive and everybody's so goddam nice all the time and they love you love you love you but he prefers New York because he'd rather be screwed by someone who hates him—he tells me he misses me.

"When are you coming home?" he asks.

I tell him I'm not sure. I have a class on the third, so I have to be back by then, but I don't know whether I'll come home for New Year's or not.

"I've got a gig on New Year's Eve," he says. "Caroline's."

Ah-ha. Doris booted him out and broke their date for New Year's Eve and now he wants me to be there. Not that he wants me to be *with* him, he doesn't, he just wants me in the audience. "Don't talk to me," he ordered at the beginning of our whatever-it-is. "Don't come up to me afterwards. Don't say anything to me, and whatever you do, don't tell me what you think. I just want you to *be* there."

"That's nice," I say about his gig.

"Well, are you going to come?"

I tell him it depends on the weather.

"The weather?" he asks. "What's the weather got to do with anything?"

He's such a New Yorker. Michael was the first person I ever met who didn't have a driver's license, and he refuses to learn, even though I offered to teach him myself.

I remind him that I'm driving back.

"So?" he says, and I say, "So, snow. I'm going to come back the first clear day after Christmas."

He wants to know when that will be and I tell him to call a meteorologist, how should I know? I'm tired and irritated, sick of being second choice, and I suddenly understand that the way to play "hard to get" is to just not care. Another lesson learned, twenty years too late.

"Ha ha," he says, "call a meteorologist. That's good, Ginger. If you run out of stiffs, you can get a job writing jokes for Johnny Carson."

"I thought he *was* a stiff," I say and he whistles.

"Oh, boy," he says, "here she goes. Stand back, folks, here comes the Funny Biographer. She's a crypt of laughs, a corpse a minute!"

"Michael," I ask, "why are you insulting me? I thought you called to say you loooooooooved me."

"Yeah, well, I do," he says. "I just can't help myself. You're such an easy target."

Well, yes. That's me, just one big bull's-eye. I'm growing tired of it; sometimes I think the only value my life has is that of being the brunt of Michael's jokes, that, in fact, I am better known as Michael's necrophiliac girlfriend than I am as myself. Even the handful of people who read my books don't know who I am. And why should they? My books are not about *me,* in any overt sense, although of course they are about nothing *but* me in my choice of subjects, my path of exploration, my passion to discover why my women can't quite make the final push to accomplishment, why they always fail, intentionally or unconsciously, at the crucial moment. I'm not the least bit interested in women who can do, or who can't do and don't care; I am only interested in those who are tormented by their inability to do whatever it is they need so desperately to do, and that is about me. And Virginia. And, I suppose, Melanie.

Michael doesn't understand. "If you're going to have a quest," he said one time, "why don't you go looking for the Holy Grail? Why do you waste your time with a bunch of dead losers?"

"They're not losers," I told him and he said, "Oh, yeah, then why haven't I heard of any of them?"

It was the perfect opportunity for me to return one of his cheap shots with a "That doesn't mean much, coming from someone who's never heard of George Eliot," to which he would reply, "Who's he?" but I restrained myself, knowing the only thing it would be good for was a mild chuckle at a faculty meeting, and since, unlike Michael, I don't plot my entire life around the effect my lame jokes will have, I didn't think it was worth it, especially since he wouldn't even get it.

He's telling me about this great new bit he's got for Caroline's and I wonder what I'm doing, continuing this silly whatever-it-is. What am I doing with Michael, I wonder. He can't swim, he can't drive, he's never read *Middlemarch*. His red-hot fame is due almost entirely to humiliating me in public.

"I think you should marry Doris," I say.

"What?" he says, as surprised as I am to hear me say that, but it suddenly seems like the right thing for him to do, for all of us.

"I said, 'I think you should marry Doris.' Soon. Why don't you get married at Caroline's on New Year's Eve? That would be cute."

"I hate it when you're patronizing," he says.

I tell him I'm not being patronizing. "I'm being serious," I say. "I think you should marry Doris and put an end to this crosstown pad-hopping. You're driving us all crazy."

"But what about us?" he asks.

"What *about* us? What do we have? Nothing. You won't even let me *say* the word 'relationship.' If I call it anything other than our 'whatever-it-is,' you disappear. If I can't define it, I don't want it. I don't want anything I can't call by its name."

"How about 'Bruno'?" he says.

"How about 'goodbye'?" I ask and hang up.

I don't bother to move. I know the phone will ring, almost instantly, he has redial on his phone. He'll say he's sorry for making a joke, it wasn't the right time. Depending upon how serious his rift with Doris is, he might even concede to allowing me to call our whatever-it-is a relationship, but I think it's too late even for that. What do I want with a man who takes the crosstown bus to my apartment to screw me and then starts singing "The Wanderer" as he's leaving?

"I'm sorry," he says when I pick up the phone. "My timing was bad."

"Michael," I say, "that's all you ever think about. Your timing. Your delivery. The effect you're having on your audience."

"That's my job," he says and I tell him I know that, I'm just not sure I want to be a part of his job anymore. I'd rather be a part of his life.

"You are a part of my life, Ginger," he says, so softly I can barely hear him and my heart melts. Whenever Michael shows the least bit of vulnerability, I turn to mush even though I know there's a good chance it's not real, that I will respond to his little-boy-lost only to get socked in the jaw for my efforts.

I don't know what to do; I don't know what I think, what I feel, what I want. So I do what all cowards do: I put it off. I say, "Michael, can we talk about this when I get back?" and he says yes, because he's a coward too. We'll put it off and put it off and put it off until one day he'll disappear for good, he'll get on the M65 and never look back and I'll bury myself with my dead losers, hoping that eventually they'll teach me how to live.

13

"IT'S MINE," VIRGINIA SAYS WHEN I HANG UP THE PHONE, "you can't have it."

She's speaking of India's life. She's standing at the top of the stairs, surrounded by a bunch of dusty old boxes, all that remains of India.

"I don't want it," I tell her for the millionth time, but for some insane reason, it's important for her to think she's taking something away from me, snatching it from my grasping claws. It gives it more value, I suppose, if she thinks someone else wants it, it gives her a reason to begin, and she has to have a reason, simply wanting to do it isn't enough.

If I wanted to write India's life, I have enough information right now, without even having to dirty my hands going through those old boxes, to write a cursory life, the unauthorized version, the one with all the dirt and none of the substance, the fraud unmasked, et cetera, et cetera, but that doesn't interest me. What does interest me about India's life is the part we know nothing about, and, unless Virginia manages to unearth some long-lost friend in Paris or London or Madrid, someone who knew the real India, the lonely, frightened woman who lived in furnished rooms and ate alone, who spent all her time making up the life she would present to us in her letters and rare visits, living, in essence, for the thrill her fictions would produce for us, unless Virginia can find a witness who knew *that* India, there is no evidence that she existed. She would never have kept a diary detailing the truth of her life, for if she hadn't needed to believe the lies, she never would have made them up in the first place.

"Yes, you do," Virginia says. "You're just waiting for me to die so you can take Mother's life and leave me out of it."

"I wouldn't do that," I tell her. "Even if I wanted to write her life, which I don't, I wouldn't leave you out."

She doesn't believe me. "Well, I'm putting it in my will," she says. "If I don't finish it before I die, which might be soon, I want all her papers burned. And mine as well."

"Fine," I tell her, "I'll toss them in the fire myself."

"Yes," she says. "You do that. And have Cease help you. You two can have a wienie roast over the ashes of my mother." She pauses. "And me."

It's the day before Christmas, she will remain in this maudlin state until the holidays are over. She will regale us with stories of holiday deaths—"Did you know that more people commit suicide on Christmas than any other day?" she'll ask on Christmas morning, as we settle into our favorite chairs for the annual unwrapping frenzy, and Poppy will say, "That's because they were lonely. People who kill themselves on Christmas are people who are alone. Aren't we lucky to be together?" And he'll smile happily and rip open the package on his lap and hold up the pajamas from Cease or the sweater from me or the suit jacket from Virginia, grinning into Cease's video recorder and mouthing, "Just what I always wanted," as if it were still 1956 and there was no sound. After we've finished with the presents, Virginia will drag out the photographs of Christmas Past and point to little Roger, "The Dead Brother," as Cease calls him, and we'll have to hear about how she "killed" him, how he was choking on the Lego piece and she grabbed him and started pounding on his back and shaking him until she shook the life right out of him.

A few years ago I suggested we forgo the Christmas ceremonies, the gift giving and the huge meal. "Christmas is for children," I said, "and since there are no children here anymore, why don't we just donate presents to the Salvation Army and have a meal out?" Poppy was horrified, not at the idea of giving presents to poor kids, he thought that was a good idea, so good, in fact, that he established the Cecil Augustus Moore Gift Drive, donating twenty-five thousand dollars as seed money. He got the Rotary and the Chamber of Commerce and the *Herald Ledger* involved, and now it's a big deal, there's a drop box at Wally's on the north end and at Peterson's downtown, where people can toss in a gift or two for "Cecil's Kids," and on Christmas afternoon, after we've finished our own exchange of gifts, he dresses up in his Santa suit and drives over to The Home and distributes presents to a bunch of sullen, unhappy adolescents who want to know why they didn't get a leather jacket. Originally, he wanted us to go along, he wanted Virginia to dress up as Mrs. Claus and Cease and me to be elves, which might have been fun thirty years ago but was out of the question now. I do sometimes go with him, more to be a witness to his generosity than for anything else. It's not enough to get his picture in the paper with some furious little moppet on his lap, he needs someone from the family present, to see how beloved he is, to take the story back and tell it at dinner, so he can be the hero of the day without seeming self-serving.

If I sound cynical it isn't because I belittle Poppy's generosity, which is real enough, or because I think the kids at The Home ungrateful—they're juvenile delinquents, locked in their barred rooms at night, abandoned and bitter and scared to death, why *should* they be overjoyed upon receiving somebody else's Chutes and Ladders? To Poppy, however, they're not little criminals; he's still living in the past, when The Home was an orphanage, and I think in his mind all the children will be rescued by wonderful childless couples, taken into their nice safe homes, and loved into good citizenship, all their little scars healed by the abundance and warmth a Good Family provides.

It isn't that Poppy doesn't know the truth. After all, he's a lawyer, he was still practicing when the county turned The Home into a detention center, when they put the bars on the windows and the locks on the doors, when they shipped the orphans out to foster homes, he even, more than likely, had a client or two in there, but in order for the story to work, for him, they must be orphans, poor helpless innocent orphans, rather than the shoplifters and car thieves they are, and since North Bay no longer has an orphanage, this will have to do. It wouldn't be the same, driving all over the county to foster homes to dole out gifts to the "real" orphans, let the Catholics do that, Poppy needs an audience, a large one. "And a captive one," Cease says.

"Your father still hasn't gotten me that typewriter," Virginia says. "I think he's jealous."

"Maybe he's waiting for Christmas," I suggest but she

wants to think he's trying to thwart her, to keep her down, to oppress her.

I offer her mine, but that won't do, she wants her own, not someone's hand-me-down and besides, it's the principle of the thing, she wants Poppy to acknowledge that she's serious, that she's worth the price of a typewriter, that she's got something to say.

"He never wants me to do anything," she whines. "He just wants me to be there for him, seen and not heard, the woman-behind-the-man and all that rot."

"Virginia," I say, "I don't want to hear this. Poppy is my father."

"And I'm not your mother?" she asks. "Why do you always take *his* side? Everybody always takes *his* side. I don't even *have* a side!"

"I wasn't going to tell you this," I tell her, "but he *is* getting you a typewriter for Christmas. I'm going to pick it up tonight. Does that make you happy?"

It's a stupid question, nothing could possibly make Virginia happy.

"Why don't you ever take my side?" she asks, pretending she didn't hear me. "You're supposed to be such a feminist, how come you don't take the woman's side?"

"The woman's side of what?"

"The woman's side in general. *My* side. Everybody thinks your father is the nicest man in the world. 'Oh, you're so lucky, Virginia,' they always say, 'being married to Cecil, he's so good to you.' And then they feel sorry for him because I'm a drunk. 'Poor Cecil,' they say, 'he's the nicest man in North Bay and he's married to that shrew Virginia, whatever did he do to deserve that?' as if I began my life as a shrew, as if I wanted to be a drunk, as if I wanted to kill my own child, as if I wanted to ruin my children's lives, as if I willfully set out to shrivel everything I touch. It's true, you know, I do, I tried to have a garden, like everybody else, I really did try, I planted peonies and tulips and bluebells and hollyhocks and all kinds of things and every single one of them shriveled up and died, all I had to do was look at them and they'd turn brown and wither away . . ."

I watch as she disappears into the wasteland of self-pity and I wish there was something I could do. I wish I could grab a length of clothesline and devise some kind of lasso, toss it around her, shout "Yahoo!" and drag her back to life, but I can't. Once the cycle has begun there is nothing to do but let it run its course, like a vicious flu, watching helplessly as she feverishly attacks herself, lays siege to herself, to prevent anyone else from doing so. It's as if she thinks that if she pummels herself into a quivering mass of guilt and remorse, lying on the floor half-dead, no one could possibly have the heart to kick her. And she's right. Even Cease relents when she gets out the metaphorical butcher knife and begins chopping at herself, he flees to his room and shuts the door, remaining there, hidden away with his childhood toys, until it's over, until she comes crawling up out of the pit, covered with her own slime, and says, "What's everybody staring at?"

I have made a study of sorts on the subject of self-pity, not because I find it compelling, but because it plays an uncomfortably large part in my life. Not only is Virginia a Grand Master, but most of my women have either suffered from it or spent a great deal of time pretending *not* to suffer from it, avoiding it by ridiculing it, fleeing from it, hardening themselves to the merest hint of its presence in anyone else. And of course I have my own share of it, which I find distressing—I would like to be one of those buoyant types who not only rise to the surface when they've been tossed into an ocean of woe, but who burst forth like some kind of cheerful rocket, landing on the beach, happy and dry and ready for the next ride Life offers to take them on, but I'm not. I'm a sinker, and although I don't dress myself in a cement overcoat to sink all the faster, as Virginia does, I'm not very gracious about it, either.

It's a kind of emotional leprosy, I suppose, and if anyone sees you have it they run like the wind before you have a chance to rub your sores all over them, as if it were catching, as if breathing the same air as a sad sack would turn them into one, and to be honest about it, I feel the same way, even though I ought to know better, even though I know I can't be tainted by it. My inclination is to run, or, in the case of my subjects, to just ignore that chapter and skip ahead to happier times. I suppose it's so terrifying because it's something we all suffer from, it's a place we all know, and one we'd rather not return to, not necessarily because it's so uncomfortable to *be* in, although it certainly is that, but because we know how ugly it looks from the outside. I think the hysterical fear of it, however, is typically American. It seems to me, from my rather limited experience, that other cultures are much more tolerant of the unattractive emotions, less frantic to "cure" them, get rid of them, flee from them, lock them away. That's why I so love nineteenth-century Russian novels—all the characters are constantly beating their breasts and pulling their hair and running off to dance all night with the gypsies and threatening to kill themselves or the Czar and nobody thinks anything of it, nobody tells Pierre to "get a life" when he starts ranting about Napoleon, about Free Masonry, about freeing the serfs, they don't try to shuffle him off to the sanatorium, they just shake their heads and say, "Well, that's how he is," and wait till he comes out of it.

Unfortunately, I am an American, as intolerant as anyone else, and I can't watch this. I stand up and tell Virginia I'm going for a walk.

"That's right," she says. "desert me in my hour of need."

Every hour is your hour of need, I don't say. Instead, I turn away and walk to the coatrack.

"You never did love me," she sniffs. "You always hated me. You have no heart."

I tell her I'm not going to have this argument with her, we've had it a million times, I don't hate her and that's that.

"But you don't love me, either," she says. "Maybe you don't hate me, but you don't love me. At least I loved my mother, and I had every reason not to."

It would be so easy to say, "Virginia, I *do* love you," but I can't. I choke on the words when they're just in my head, not even anywhere near my mouth. I know I can't do it, so I don't even try.

If she could just say, "Please don't go," I wouldn't. I would force myself to stay and watch her tear herself to pieces, to be the witness she so desperately needs, not to help her or cure her or even console her, but simply to *see* what it feels like to be inside her skin, to live with what she has to live with, to feel what she feels. If she could ask me to do that, I would, that is the arbitrary price I've placed on it, I will watch her suffering but only if she asks and, by asking, acknowledges that watching is just as painful to me as slashing herself is to her.

"You don't care about anybody but yourself," she says. "That's why you can't keep a man, that's why you'll never have children, you're just too selfish. I always said you were born without a heart and I was right."

I don't try to defend myself, there is no defense that I can make that would stand up to her fury, which has little to do with me.

"All you care about is your 'work,'" she says. "You're just like Mother, and you're going to end up just like her, too, dead and forgotten, nothing but a bunch of papers in a box, lying out on the street waiting for the garbage man to come and get it because you won't even have anybody who will care enough to keep you alive."

I hear her words but they don't get in. She hurls them at me, sharp and deadly, but they bounce off, like rubber-tipped arrows, falling impotent at my feet. The truth is, I can't feel them. I haven't had a feeling of any depth since Virginia killed Fritz. Not that I blame that particular trauma for numbing my ability to feel, it's simply that that was the last time I allowed anything to get to me.

"Virginia," I say, "why don't you get dressed and come with me, a walk would do you good."

"Don't try to change the subject," she says. "You're just like your father."

"We can take a nice long walk along the beach," I suggest, "and then go downtown and have lunch at Snyder's. Just like old times."

"Snyder's is closed," she says. "Cockroaches."

"Well, we can go somewhere else. Do you want to go or not?"

She shakes her head, like an inconsolable child, and the tears run silently down her gray, lined face. I am struck, simultaneously, by two horrible thoughts: first, how ugly and old she looks; second, how glad I am that Michael can't see her, can't look at her and see the future me, and I am overwhelmed with self-loathing for having such despicable thoughts. She's right, I am the most selfish person on earth, and I deserve everything awful that happens to me.

She continues to weep, noiselessly, her head slowly lowering into her chest, as if she were trying to curl up into a little ball. I would give anything, anything, to be able to run across the room and throw my arms around her and tell her I love her, but I can't, I am paralyzed, in that kind of semi-nightmare state in which I want to move but can't, as if some invisible force is pushing me down, holding my arms and legs rigid even though I want desperately to break free.

She looks up at me. "Go on," she snaps, waving her hand at the door, "get out of my house," and I am released, I can move, and I run for the door.

14

"WHY DON'T YOU STOP THINKING ABOUT LIFE AND JUST LIVE
it?" Michael once asked, and I should have ended our whatever-it-is right then, for it was obvious that I would never get
any sympathy from someone who could ask such a stupid
question. If I could, I would, and it wouldn't be an issue.
What could be more obvious?

I don't like to think about what stops me from living, so I
think about what stops other people instead. The closest I've
come to an answer, for myself or anyone else, is cowardice.
And I don't mean that timorous, wilting-violet, hedgehog
kind of cowardice, the kind one sees all the time in New
York, those women who walk down the street tightly clutching their handbags and constantly looked wide-eyed over
their shoulders, as if every passer-by were out to "get" them.
Neither I nor any of my women are creampuffs, but we all

seem to have some sort of deep-rooted fear that keeps us paralyzed, unable to make the final push. I suppose it is a kind of moral cowardice, and I don't like to think about that. I would like to think that given the opportunity I could be brave and strong and good, but I have never been tested, and I am terrified that when I am, I will fail.

I look at my own life, and the lives of my women, and wonder why—why are we cowards? What are we afraid of? There is nothing horrendous in any of our lives to have caused such fearfulness.

I remember a day, years ago, when I was on my way to see Greta; it was one of those wonderful bright winter days, with just a touch of warmth in the air. The sky was that incredible pastel blue in which all the buildings stand out and glimmer, flat and two-dimensional, as if the city itself had stopped for a moment, to enjoy the beauty of the world, as if it was held in suspension, like a photograph. As I walked along Greta's street, I saw two women leaning out of an open window while a man, standing on the sidewalk across the street, flirted with them. There was a large, shiny patch of ice on the sidewalk and suddenly the man began dancing on it, doing a kind of combination soft-shoe and Hans Brinker skate step, and the women laughed with delight and I was overwhelmed with the desire to go dance with him, to run down the sidewalk and slide across the ice, to dance and sing with this stranger who was so happy to be alive, to cast off the Judges, who were already stumbling around in my head, pulling on their robes and adjusting their wigs and grumbling about dignity and propriety and wasn't I too old for this and maybe the man didn't *want* anyone else barging in on his fun, it wasn't as if he had *invited* me to join him, maybe he was trying to pick up one of the women and I would ruin his chance and he'd scream at me, so that by the time I reached him I could barely raise my head to return his smile. The

Judges patted each other on the back and congratulated each other on a job well done and retired happily to their chambers, having nipped another threat to their omnipotence in the bud.

The hallmark of the coward is regret, and, being a coward, I have my share of regrets, but I think the thing I regret most of all is not standing up to the Judges that day. I am thoroughly ashamed of myself for passively allowing them to browbeat me into suppressing that tiny spark of spontaneity, snuffing it out before it had a chance to grow bright, bright enough for me to see them as the bugaboos they are. It's a silly thing, I know, especially when I have so many greater things to regret, so many things I wanted to try but didn't because I was afraid I would fail; so many adventures I wanted to take but didn't because I was afraid of the unknown; so many things I wanted to say but was struck dumb because I was afraid no one would listen; so many people I wanted to love but couldn't because I was afraid I wouldn't be loved in return.

I have a trunkful of regrets and yet the only one I carry around with me is that of not dancing on the ice that day; it's the one that has taken on significance, as if for one fleeting second Desire had grabbed me by the hand and said, "Come! Don't be afraid!" and I refused to go. It was my one chance to banish the Judges forever and all I had to do was follow my desire, run down the sidewalk and dance across the ice before they even knew what was happening, and I didn't do it. I somehow knew that I had irrevocably changed my life that day and as I walked past the man, smiling wanly at him, I realized I had, in a matter of seconds, turned from young to old, that Desire would never bother with me again, I was a lost cause, I would forever be paralyzed by my fear of being censured. Up to that point, I had thought I would have an endless stream of opportunities; it was just that the time wasn't right, I needed to build up my confidence, win a few awards, get on a tenure track, be safely ensconced in a loving relationship, lose weight, get a haircut, but the next chance that came along, I'd take, if only I had even one of the above. I never dreamed that there would come a time when there wasn't a next chance, that instead of growing bolder I would simply begin to grow more cowardly. It never occurred to me that Blake was right, that if I turned her down too often, Desire would simply disappear.

If character is fate (or destiny, depending on the translation) then are we doomed to paralysis forever? Is cowardice an ineradicable character defect or a learned behavior, one that can be changed given the right environment? Is character itself immutable or malleable? One can change one's behavior, one's attitude, one's beliefs, but is it within the realm of possibility to change one's character? If one is, for example, a coward, and one hates being a coward, truly despises his or her cowardice, tries everything imaginable to be brave and courageous and fails miserably at every turn, is it sane to keep trying, to keep failing, to keep hating oneself when it may not even be within human potential to change it? Of course, being an American, and an American of a certain age, it seems almost blasphemous to think that there is anything beyond the reach of Free Will, that there is anything that cannot be won by hard work, determination, and persistence.

Not that I'm an expert on psychology; I'm not. Nor am I an "expert" on anything; in fact, I am woefully ignorant, despite the fact that I pass for an educated person, that I am, indeed, "educated," that I could, if I were jerky enough and insecure enough to do so, insist that people address me as "Dr. Moore." Sadly, my being "educated" doesn't mean much, there is too much information, it's an enormous task simply to keep up with the information in one's own field, much less have anything other than the most cursory knowledge of any subject outside of it.

I have a little Faustian fantasy, in which Mephistopheles comes to me to make a deal and I ask him for knowledge. "I want to know everything," I tell him and he shakes his head and tells me I'm too ignorant for him to even begin, to fill the gaps would be a task too difficult even for the Devil himself. He offers me a million dollars and my own talk show instead, but I turn him down, I'm not interested in selling my soul for a few lousy bucks and the opportunity to moderate the public humiliations of an endless stream of exhibitionists.

As far as I'm concerned, the only difference between the talk shows of today and the stocks of the eighteenth century is that the people who go on talk shows humiliate themselves by choice; they willingly offer themselves up to the rage and the booing and hissing of the studio audience, just for the privilege of sitting in front of a camera, for the opportunity to live forever on tape. I doubt that any eighteenth-century wife beater or child molester or adulterer or coven member would have gone willingly to the stocks, or that Hester Prynne would have gladly worn her scarlet A if she knew Nathaniel Hawthorne would make her famous. And we, the audience? Well, we're just like those nasty villagers we love to hate in the movies, those small-minded, petty, tight-faced Puritans with their baskets full of rotten vegetables and cow dung, the people we think we would never be. Sitting in the warmth of a twentieth-century movie theater, we think we would be better, we would stand up for Hester, or whomever, we would never be like those people, ready to pelt the miscreant as soon as he's locked in, and yet we sit in our living rooms, pelting verbally at the TV screen or calling some 800-number to pelt on the phone.

Virginia thinks the people who go on talk shows are actors. It is inconceivable to her that anyone would go on nationwide TV and talk about their inability to achieve orgasm or their love for a serial killer. She'll sit in front of the tube all day, laughing hysterically, occasionally calling me up and asking me why I don't try to get a job writing for one of the talk shows. "They must need a lot of writers," she says, "to come up with this stuff."

If Virginia finds something baffling she simply refuses to believe it's real. "Someone made that up," she'll declare, and as far as she's concerned, most of modern life is just someone's mad fantasy. I too find our world baffling but it is its very realness that bewilders me.

This is why I prefer not only the dead to the living but the past to the present. It isn't, I don't think, that I'm a reactionary, although Michael claims I am. I have no illusions about the past; I don't want to go back to a "happier time" that really wasn't any "happier" than our own; in fact, the past I'm visiting right now, Charlotte Cibber's eighteenth-century London slum, is filthy and brutal, filled with crime and gin houses and despair, a world in which the rich think nothing of driving their carriages through the streets, right over the dirty little urchins, oops, well, one less brat in the world. Entertainment, for the masses, consisted of packing up a picnic lunch and going out to Tyburn to watch the cut-purses get hanged.

For me, the allure of the past—and I'm speaking here of the past in general and not my own past, which I visit as infrequently as possible—is that it remains the same forever. Not even the revisionists can change history, they can only, if they're successful, change our consciousness of it. History itself remains static, and I find that incredibly comforting. I may go to sleep at night wondering what the next day will bring, what new discovery or development will blast into my life, rendering me and my world obsolete, but at least I know the past will remain exactly as it was, that I can pick up Charlotte's apologia and she will be sitting exactly where I left her, in front of her pitiful little fire, with her mangy spaniel at her feet and her parrot perched on the armoire, squawking "Bilbo's the word!" for all eternity.

If that makes me a reactionary, well, then I'm guilty. I'm not anti-progress, or anti-change; in fact, I think we have a long way to go before we reach a point where we can truly call ourselves "civilized"; it's just that I'm anti-mindlessness of any sort, mindless progress seems as idiotic to me as mindless regression.

But I digress. I could go on and on—one of my favorite fantasies is that of being a pundit. I would love to be asked my opinion on absolutely everything, but nobody cares what I think; the only people who ever ask my opinion are my students, and all they want to know is whether I think my agent will take their manuscript.

15

"ASK ME WHAT I THINK," I SAY AT DINNER.

"What you think about *what?*" Virginia asks.

"Anything," I say and turn to Cease. "It's a new game we can play. 'Family Pundit.' And I'll start. Ask me something."

"How come you get to start?" he asks.

"Is that a real question, or are you just being difficult?"

"Real," he says.

"Okay. I get to start because I made up the game. Next question—but make it something important, something that matters."

Virginia wants to know if it has to be something I know about and I say no. "The point is to be convincing," I explain, "to make it sound as if you know about it."

"Wait!" Cease cries. "I've got a better idea. Let's all write down questions and put them in the middle of the table and then we all have to come up with opinions on them and the one who sounds the most convincing wins that round and the one who wins the most rounds gets to be Family Pundit."

"Like the Dictionary Game!" Poppy says and he and Virginia agree that Cease's is a better idea and I grudgingly give in—it *is* more fair—even though we'll all end up voting for ourselves and I had been hoping to have the floor to myself for once. Virginia gets up and rifles through the junk drawer for a packet of ancient recipe cards we can use for our questions while the rest of us make space beside our plates.

"The family that proclaims together, remains together," Poppy declares and we all laugh dutifully.

"That's good, Cecil," Virginia says as she hands out the cards, and Poppy beams.

I still can't believe this childlike old man is my father. Virginia has been complaining for years that Poppy was "losing his marbles," but I never paid much attention to her; she isn't wrapped too tight herself and I only half-listen when she starts babbling over the phone. I see him annually, for a week or two, and other than the whitening hair and the age spots and the stoop that makes him appear so much smaller than he was, he has seemed much the same over the years, a little sillier perhaps, but I thought that was my fault, that I had outgrown his jokes and his goofy names, that I no longer found them cute and endearing, not because they weren't but because I had grown humorless and curmudgeonly.

He had always seemed so brilliant to me. I adored him; I worshipped him—he was so tall and dapper, sitting on the porch in the summer, having his morning coffee, dressed in the grey linen suit Virginia had picked out for him, with his silk tie dripping down his chest like a strip of morning sky. He seemed so wise, so all-knowing, so inducted into the secrets of the world, and I could only gaze in wonder and awe at his power. "Did you see this?" he'd ask Virginia, waving the newspaper at her while she sat there, staring blank-eyed out the screen, and when she'd refuse to answer he'd turn to me, as if I were an adult, as if I were truly capable of understanding, as if my opinion mattered, and ask me what I thought about Sputnik. I didn't think anything at all about Sputnik, except that it sounded vaguely unclean, like some thing you'd find at the bottom of a toilet bowl, but that didn't matter. What mattered was that he was talking to *me,* noticing *me,* and I was glad Virginia didn't answer him.

It's all very Freudian, I know—Electra run amok. I often wonder what the world would be like if Freud had never existed, if we weren't all such incorrigible amateur psychologists. I'm as bad as anyone else, worse, perhaps. Everyone is a study to me, I dice up and splay everybody who walks into my life, I examine them for the more obvious psychological patterns, I seize them and size them up and pretend I know them, pretend I understand them better than they understand themselves, pretend I recognize their true motivations when the truth is, I know nothing, I can no more see into anyone else's heart than they can see into mine. The best any of us can do is guess.

"Here's my question," Poppy says, tossing his card. It falls into the dusty arrangement of dried flowers and wooden fruit that passes for a centerpiece and he carefully picks it out and lays it, face down, next to the butter dish. He leans over and tries to see what Virginia is writing but she jerks her arm over her card. Cease is chuckling ominously and I realize, too late, that this game is a mistake. I should have just arrived at the dinner table and begun ranting, forcing my opinions down their throats along with the chicken cacciatore. But in our family it's impossible to approach anything serious outside the context of "fun"; anything one says is grist for the joke mill and the closest one can come to serious, without being humiliated, is ironic.

"I'm ready," Virginia says and places her card, face down, under Poppy's. Cease waits for me to put mine in the pile and then leans back in his chair and says, "Okay, I'll start."

"No," Poppy says, "let Ginger start. It's her game, she should go first."

I just want it to be over, but I reach for a card, not Cease's and read: "Earlier this year, Coleman Young claimed that there were terrorist groups forming in the suburbs, arming themselves in preparation to invade Detroit. What do you think this means?"

"Nonsense," Virginia says.

"Is that your opinion?" I ask and she nods.

"Short and sweet," Poppy says. "I'll go next." He's ready; it was his question, one he's probably been debating with the lawyers down at the office. He pulls his chair closer to the table and looks us each in the eye, as if he were preparing to soften, or enrage, a jury.

"Coleman Young," he says softly, "was a good mayor. A fine mayor. Possibly even a great mayor." He pauses for effect, as if to let us savor Coleman Young's tragedy. "Consider the things he did for Detroit. The Renaissance Center. Joe Louis Arena. The Riverfront. Detroit was practically a ghost town and he revitalized it, brought people together, people of all races." He makes his voice shake, as if he were going to start crying, as if he were personally heartbroken by the tragedy he is about to describe. "But the fact of the matter is, Coleman Young has lost his marbles."

Cease giggles and Poppy shakes a pudgy finger at him. "Oh, no, it's not funny," he says. "It is a tragedy worthy of the great writers. Shakespeare. Sophocles. O'Neill."

Virginia rolls her eyes at me. "As if he's ever read them," she mouths.

"The evidence," Poppy continues, "is overwhelming. The palace guard. The secrecy. His disappearances. And now, this.

This is, sadly, just another piece of evidence that proves he is incapable of governing. The idea of Grosse Pointe house-wives arming themselves with semiautomatic weapons and launching an invasion force in their Cadillacs, driving down Gratiot in a convoy headed for Jefferson, is lunacy." He shakes his head sadly, as if he wished he didn't have to say what he was about to say. "The man is nuts," he murmurs. "Impeach him."

Virginia claps politely and Poppy smiles, sure he'll win round one.

"Your turn," he says to me.

"Frankly," I begin, "I think that while the reality of Grosse Pointers arming themselves to invade Detroit is rather ludi-crous, the underlying *feeling* is probably quite accurate. The mayor's fear is actually a metaphor for the feeling of not just being invaded but of being annihilated . . ."

"Bleeding heart, bleeding heart," Cease chants. "Can't we have a time limit?" He asks Virginia for an egg timer, but she doesn't have one.

"I'm not finished," I say. "This is important, it really makes sense if you think about it," but I'm overruled.

"Thank you, Comrade Ginger," Poppy says, giggling.

Cease thinks someone should just nuke Detroit and start all over again. "Ten-second urban renewal," he says and I'm horrified.

"How can you say something so horrible, even in jest?" I ask, but that's not part of the game, Cease says, as if it were his game rather than mine, no rebuttals.

"Okay, let's do my question," he says and I say wait, we have to vote on the first round.

It's a tie, as I knew it would be, we all vote for ourselves.

"Forget it," I say, "this isn't going to work."

"I want to ask my question," Cease insists, but I don't think it's a good idea.

Virginia stands up and starts removing the dishes from the table. "I don't like this game," she says. "And besides, it's almost time for my program."

Poppy says it wasn't as much fun as he thought it would be, but he pats me on the back and tells me it was a nice try.

"Wait," Cease says, but Poppy says he has to go to work on his book.

"I'm on page 578," he tells me. "What do you think of that? None of your books is longer than four hundred pages."

Poppy leaves and Cease grabs his card and begins reading loudly: "A Seattle man who shot, killed, and dismembered his entire family was acquitted by a jury on the grounds that he had been influenced by an episode of *Kojak*. Do you think this will result in a rash of copy-cat murders?"

"Not here, I hope," Virginia says and Cease says, "Is that your answer? Is that your *opinion*?"

"What do you want me to say, dear? 'Oh! I hope you're not planning to dismember *us*!'"

Cease jumps up and grabs his coat from the rack next to the mudroom door. "I'm going out," he growls and Virginia says, "Have a good time, dear. Don't murder anyone while you're out."

He slams the door and Virginia sighs.

"He made it up," she says. "He just made it up to shock me. But I wouldn't put it past him. There's something wrong with someone who would want you to think he might murder you in your sleep." Virginia thinks it was Cease's two years in Vietnam that turned him into a nut case, but the truth is, he fell apart when Virginia did and he's never quite recovered.

"He says he's in therapy," I say and Virginia snorts.

"Therapy, schmerapy, all that's good for is making him think it's 'okay' to do whatever it was he was going to do in the first place. And to make everybody blame me, if he does turn out to be a murderer. They always blame the mother, the mother is always too something, too cold or too suffocating or too remote or too overbearing or, in my case, too drunk."

"You don't really think Cease could ever hurt anyone, do you?" I ask and she shrugs.

"No," she says, "he's all sound and fury. Of course, there *was* a murder in my family, I remember Florida and Asia talking about it, some second cousin twice removed shot some other kind of cousin over a horse, or a woman, it doesn't matter which, a horse and a woman being of about equal value back then, and the one who killed the other ran away to Texas and founded another branch of the family, the one that ended up being rich. I think his great-grandson is a senator or something."

She sighs and tells me I was smart to be an Old Maid.

"Thanks," I say and she assures me it wasn't meant as an insult.

"Being a mother isn't all it's cracked up to be," she says. "No matter what you do, your children will end up hating you and if that's all you've done with your life, you can't help wondering why you were alive, what use have you been if the only thing you've accomplished is warping your own offspring?"

"Oh, Virginia, don't start . . ." I begin, but she waves her hands about in the air, as if she were scattering a swarm of gnats hovering around her face.

"Don't 'Oh, Virginia' me," she says. "It's true, and I know it's true, and there's nothing anybody can do about it. I certainly can't make it up to you and Cease, just as my mother couldn't make it up to me for casting me off like an old shoe, dumping me with those old hags as if I were a foundling. Do you know what they used to call me?"

I shake my head.

"India's 'biological droppings.' At night, when I was supposed to be asleep, I'd go out on to the balcony and listen to them carping down in the parlor, complaining about Mother, complaining about how hard their lives were and it didn't make it any easier that Mother had run off to Europe and left them to take care of her 'biological droppings.'"

"That must have been awful," I say and she glares at me.

"Of course it was awful. But I never blamed Mother for my problems. In fact, I admired her, she did what she wanted with her life, which is more than I can say for myself."

"What is it you wanted to do?" I ask, rather cruelly, for that's not the point. I don't think Virginia had anything specific in mind, not even during her tenure as a Person, she just wanted More, More than who she was and More than what she had and the ways in which she might have attained that were incidental. Because she was nothing, she could have been anything.

She doesn't answer. "Therapy," she says. "Whatever happened to respect? Whatever happened to conscience? Whatever happened to the fear of God?"

These are questions I wished she would have asked when we were playing Family Pundit but it's too late now, she's got her drink and a fresh pack of cigarettes and she's switching on the TV, gazing around the kitchen in a kind of daze, as if she were lost, searching for a place to make herself comfortable now that she's been banished from the den by the Christmas tree.

"I think I'll go downtown," I tell her and she nods as the studio audience begins chanting, "Wheel! . . . of! . . . FOR-TUNE!" and I wonder if, when she's alone, in her den, with the door closed and drapes pulled, when no one can see or hear her, she chants along, as if she hoped the wheel might turn a few more times for her, as if she hoped there was still a chance for her to hit the jackpot.

16

DOWNTOWN NORTH BAY IS PRACTICALLY DESERTED; MOST of the last-minute shoppers are out at the new mall at the north end of town, a horrid sterile depressing place filled with chain shops and angry, determined-looking women dressed in sweatpants and spandex, furiously trying to speed-walk through the dallying shoppers. Even the Salvation Army Santas have deserted downtown, preferring the heated vestibules of the mall, and I miss the sound of their big brass bells ringing along the street.

It's a ghost town. The bright lights from the shop windows shine out on the snowdrifts along the edge of the sidewalk but they illuminate only the eerie darkness, and if I didn't know North Bay I would be afraid, afraid of the emptiness, of what might be lurking behind the boarded-up doorways. But I'm not, the ghosts that inhabit downtown North Bay are friendly, and I remember the joy with which I'd come downtown at night during the week before Christmas, running from store to store in the snow, clambering over the snowdrifts with arms full of packages, running to the car to load it up and then to shop some more. Everyone was so happy, wrapped up like Christmas presents themselves, their eyes bright from the cold. It was like a huge party, and in every store I was sure to find some friends and we'd all go to Penelope's Candy Shoppe for hot chocolate or the Coney Island for coneys and fries, and show each other our loot, filled with the excitement and happiness of our generosity.

Now the streets are silent, except for the Christmas carols coming from Peterson's PA system, and I find it all very sad. The Downtown North Bay Association has made a desperate attempt to lure customers back by restoring their buildings to their nineteenth-century grandeur, by having ice sculpture contests and horse-drawn sleighs and making their sales clerks dress up in Victorian clothes, and while that has worked elsewhere, the North Bayites aren't buying it; they will take warmth over charm any day, and stay away in droves.

I feel old, ancient, as musty and forgotten as my women, overwhelmed by my inability to feel comfortable in my own world, or rather, in any of my worlds. In Michael's world I feel old and stodgy and rigid, unsophisticated and pathetically unhip; in my professional world I feel inadequate and slightly stupid, somehow illegitimate, afraid that at any moment I will be unmasked for the fraud I am. Here, in my childhood home, where I should at least be able to bask in the relative comfort of the familiar, I feel discarded, as if my childhood and youth had been not only usurped by the new generation but obliterated by it.

Michael's right, I'm too Germanic. I take these things much too seriously, it's as if what is merely a fleeting sense of personal loss and sorrow takes on some sort of global significance when in fact it means nothing, except that at this particular point in time people prefer malls to downtown shops, and five years from now the reverse might be true, I'll come back here and the sidewalks will be jammed with people and I'll be complaining about how impossible it is to find a parking place.

"Ginger!" a voice calls. "Ginger Moore!"

I stop and look around, but I see no one I recognize—the few people on the street are wrapped up like neon mummies, with their bright-colored parkas and their ski caps pulled down over their foreheads and their scarves pulled up to their noses.

"Ginger, you dope!" the voice shouts. "Here!"

I see someone waving across the street and wonder who it could be. Only a high school classmate would call me a "dope," and I wave back tentatively, wondering if I am going to have a long conversation with someone I don't remember.

She comes bounding across the street and begins punching my arm.

"How soon we forget!" she says and I laugh and hug her.

"Melanie! How was I supposed to recognize you under all that?"

"All for one!" she shouts, thrusting out her mittened hand. "And one for all!" I answer. We pause, waiting for Maggie Pittsfield to appear out of the past, shrieking "Together we stand and united we fall!" We look around, sheepishly, and then burst into the brazen, riotous laughter of the teenagers we will always be whenever we see each other.

"How long are you staying?" she asks and I tell her I'm getting out of Dodge on the first clear day after Christmas.

"Me, too," she says, "although I don't know why I'm in such a big hurry to get back to *him*."

I ask if *he* has a name and a blush darkens her wind-pinkened cheeks as she shrugs and says, "I get them mixed up. I should only marry guys with the same name. Bob or something." She laughs. "You know, it's weird. With all the guys I've married, I've never had a Bob. Maybe next time."

"Well, how are you?" I ask and she wants to know if that means how *is* she or is she off the booze?

"Both," I say and she says she's fine and she's off the booze, ten months now, the longest she's ever gone.

"I think I'm going to make it this time," she says, and her voice begins to quiver and I put up my hand, no need to say anything, no need to apologize for the 3:00 A.M. phone calls, no need to remind herself what a jerk she was.

We're standing in front of Penelope's and I suggest we go in.

"Hot chocolate!" Melanie cries and we rush through the door. Grim little Mr. Ingram is sitting behind the candy counter, scowling and reading a book as if he hadn't moved in twenty years. We wave at him as we pass into the back, into the bright little room with the neat booths lining the walls and the chandeliers, with their candy-shaped crystals, dangling over the tables. The booths are made of rich, dark wood, cherry perhaps, worn smooth and lustrous by generations of shoppers and their children, and, on weekends, screaming preteens slurping cherry Cokes before running next door to the Iroquois Theatre, long since closed, replaced first by a men's shop, then by one of those dollar-or-less places, and now, finally, nothing. Just an empty glass window.

We begin peeling off layers of clothes as Melanie tells me about her new job.

"Are you ready for this?" she asks and I nod as I pull my sweater over my head.

"I'm working at Kroger's. As a *bagger*."

"Melanie! What on earth for?"

She shrugs. "It's what they call a 'get-sober job,' but let me tell you, if I can keep this up without going back to the bottle, I can get through anything. It's one of those stomp-out-your-ego jobs, just in case you had any left." She sighs and grabs the menu from the metal holder. "It's an okay job for some high school kid who just wants to make enough money for a junked-up old car, but for an adult, it's hell. You just wouldn't believe how cruel people are," but yes I would. I remind her that I spent several summers as a cashier at Farmer Bob's, and she says, "Yeah, but you were a *cashier.* I'm still working my way up."

We laugh and it doesn't seem so sad, as long as we're laughing.

"I tell you," she says, "I will never, as long as I live, be rude to anybody ever again. It's as if these old bags—no pun intended—saved up all their hate and take it out on the baggers, the only people in the world who have less power than they do. They call me stupid all the time—'What are you doing, stupid?' 'How can you be so stupid?' 'Don't put that in there, stupid.' The only thing that keeps me from crawling home is that I wouldn't want to give any of them the satisfaction of knowing they made me feel like a worm."

She tosses the menu aside and puts her elbows on the table, cradling her face in her hands as she looks at me.

"So," she says, "how about you? Is Michael in or out?"

"Out," I say, "or at least I think so. I think I ended it for good the other day. I told him to marry Doris."

"Ugh," Melanie says. "That slug?"

I tell her Doris isn't a "slug," but the truth of the matter is, I don't know what Doris is; in fact, I don't even know if Doris exists at all. I've never actually seen her, but the way Michael speaks of her makes me believe she *is* real, for who would create a make-believe girlfriend and then complain about how awful she is?

Melanie tells me she saw Michael on David Letterman and

he's much cuter than I made him out to be, too cute to marry a slug.

I tell her he's too cute for me, too.

"Do you really turn on the garbage disposal when you're having phone sex?" she asks.

"I don't *have* a garbage disposal," I tell her. "Nobody in New York has a garbage disposal, they're illegal. And we don't have phone sex."

"Well, you'd be crazy to let him go," she says. "He's practically *famous*. The night after he was on TV, I told everybody at work that my friend Ginger goes out with him and Linda was so impressed she promised to get me moved up to cashier with the next opening."

I tell her I'm glad he's good for something and she says I'm nuts. "You have the best life of anybody I know," she says. "You go out with a famous person, you live in New York, you have a career, you get to meet all those actors and artists and stuff. Jeez, Ginger, you've got it made. I wish I were you."

"My life's okay," I say and she says, "It beats being a bagger, that's for sure."

She thinks I should go right home and call Michael and make up with him.

"He's cute and he's funny, what more do you want?"

"I want to be appreciated," I say.

"Forget about it," she says. "I'm an expert on this, don't forget, and the two most important questions are, one, how long can I stand to look at this person? and, two, does this person *ever* make me happy? The rest of it—the sex, the love, all that crap, it gets old, it comes and goes, but if you can stand to look at him, and he makes you laugh every once in a while, you're better off than most."

"Virginia says I'm better off as an Old Maid," I tell her and she shrugs.

"I can see that," she says, "but it's not for me. I can't take the loneliness. I need somebody around who I can hate more than myself."

"That doesn't always work," I suggest and she says she knows, but it works for her, at least most of the time.

"How is Virginia, by the way?" she asks and I tell her the same as always, still drinking, still depressed, still stuck in her own mire.

"Want me to come over and do a Twelfth Step on her?" Melanie asks and I tell her no, not unless it's her duty or something, some penance she has to pay.

"You're welcome to try, but I doubt if it will do any good. And you'd have to be careful, she'd probably spike your drink."

"Just like old times," Melanie says. "Going over to your house always was an adventure."

Our hot chocolates arrive, delivered by the waitress in her pink-and-white striped candy-cane uniform and I remember how as a child the only thing I wanted from life was to be a waitress at Penelope's, to wear that lovely uniform and smile and be friendly and make people happy by giving them sundaes.

Melanie wants to know what I'm working on now and I tell her. Her eyes glaze over with a look of polite incomprehension and I feel like an idiot.

"I still think you should write a book about me," she says. "I don't plan to be a bag lady forever, you know, I'm going to *do* something with my life."

I nod and ask her if she keeps in touch with anyone else from North Bay.

She shakes her head. "I used to," she says, "but I made too many drunken phone calls. God! Remember Pinkie Inez?"

I don't.

"Yes, you do. Pinkie Inez. With the hair."

She lifts her hand and raises it above her head a few feet to indicate a massive beehive.

"Oh, okay, Pinkie," I say and Melanie blushes.

"I don't know what got into me," she says, "but for some reason I got her number from information and just started tormenting her, stupid stuff like, 'This little Pinkie went to market, this little Pinkie went wee-wee-wee all the way home,' really jerky twelve-year-old stuff. It made no sense, I had nothing against Pinkie, and we'd been pretty good friends in school. I don't know why I decided to call her, unless it was her hair, and once I started, I couldn't stop. It wasn't malicious or anything, I'd call and say something stupid and hang up and laugh my guts out. If I couldn't get in my call to Pinkie, I'd get so depressed I couldn't move, it was as if my life had condensed to two simple choices: call Pinkie and laugh or don't call her and cry.

"My phone bills were astronomical. I was calling from St. Paul, for God's sake, in the middle of the day, fifty cents a minute, just to say, 'Pinkie is a finkie,' and hang up."

She takes a sip of her chocolate, licking the whipped cream from the rim. "I got caught. They traced the calls and I would have had to come back here to go to court and face her, so I drank myself into the psych ward and Evan took care of it."

"Who's Evan?"

"My third," she says. "Evan Devon. No shit. Who would do that to a kid?"

"Anyway," she says, "that was the end of Evan." She heaves a tremendous sigh. "I suppose I should call Pinkie and apologize, although I wouldn't know how to find her. I'm sure she's got an unlisted number now."

We both laugh at poor Pinkie's expense and I look across the table and see the girl Melanie was, bright and beautiful and full of the devil, alive with hope and the determination to get everything she could out of life. "When I grow up," she used to say when we were out at the cemetery, "the one thing I will never do is cry," but I imagine she's done little else.

"You're the only one who didn't tell me to go fuck myself," she says.

"All for one . . . one for all," I say.

She leans over the table and gives me a cinnamony kiss. "I wish you were in St. Paul," she says, "or that I lived in New York. I don't really have any friends anymore."

"What about what's-his-name, your husband?" I ask. "What *is* his name?"

She suddenly becomes very serious. "Ginger, I have something to tell you," she says in that tone of voice that makes one not want to hear it. It's something awful, but I can't imagine what it could be, unless husband number five is some sort of criminal.

"What?"

"Now, promise you won't be upset."

"I won't be upset," I promise, thinking perhaps "he" is not "he" at all but "she," something that would neither surprise nor shock me but would send her pamphleteering father over the edge.

"It's Frank," she says.

"Frank who?"

"Frank Tomowitz."

"Frank?" I ask. "What's wrong with him? Where is he? What's he done? Is he dead?"

"No," she says, "he's not dead. He's in St. Paul, Ginger. That's what I'm trying to tell you, he's in St. Paul and he's the fifth Mr. Melanie Fraser."

I'm stunned. The room becomes brighter, as if suddenly lit by a kleig light, the little glass gumdrops hanging from the chandelier seem to glimmer and shake and I wonder if this is how one feels just before one faints. I have never fainted before, even when I was a kid and we'd spin around and around and then clutch each other's waists, squeezing off the air, to make each other pass out, I never did, I always remained steady, watchful, alert.

But now even the booth is spinning and I realize this is the very booth in which Frank proposed to me, he was sitting exactly where Melanie is sitting now, watching me as anxiously as he was twenty years ago. I close my eyes and tell myself none of this matters, none of this is real, my real life is in New York, nothing that happens in North Bay has any effect on my real life.

"Do you mean to tell me," I finally say, "that you're married to my ex-husband?"

She nods.

"Melanie, how *could* you? How could you call me for all those years and talk about him and never tell me him was *him*!"

"I didn't know how to tell you," she says. "I was afraid you'd be mad at me, and you were the only friend I had."

"Had" is right, I think. It's ridiculous, I know. I haven't seen Frank in over fifteen years, and we parted amicably enough. It just wasn't working and it was the seventies and so we split, as they said back then, no hard feelings, he went his way, out to California to strike it rich, and I went mine, across the ocean to London to find peace and quiet in the dark, ancient safety of the British Museum. I had always wished him well, I thought, but now I'm not so sure.

"Ginger, you're not mad, are you?" Melanie asks, and I know I shouldn't be, it's insane, we're all adults now, we're all completely different people than we were twenty years ago. In a way, it's not even as though she married my ex-husband, the Frank she married probably bears no resemblance whatsoever to the Frank I was married to, he's probably fat and bald and boring, he probably watches Rush Limbaugh and blames all the problems of the world on "homos" and "feminazis" and "welfare frauds."

"Is he fat?" I ask, and she says oh no, he looks great, that's one good thing about Frank, at least he's someone she never minds looking at. And he still makes her laugh.

"Remember how funny he was?" she asks and I look around for the waitress and signal for the check.

"If he's so hilarious, how come you were always complaining about *him*?"

She shrugs. "Habit, I guess. And, I didn't want you to know. I knew you'd be mad."

"I'm not mad," I say, grabbing the check from the waitress, "I'm just surprised. *Very* surprised. Jesus, Melanie, what did you say to him after you'd finished screaming at me for turning you into a drunk, 'Guess I told that old battle-axe'? And then did the two of you sit around making fun of me? That must have been a laugh riot."

Tears well up in her eyes. "I knew I shouldn't have told you," she says. "You would never have known the difference, but Frank wanted me to be honest with you. He said I had to make amends and I couldn't make amends if I kept on lying."

"Is he in AA, too?" I ask and she nods and wipes at her tears with her balled-up napkin.

"It's all right, Melanie," I say, reaching across the table and coldly tapping her hand. "I'm glad you're both sober and I hope you're happy."

"But you're still mad," she says. "You're leaving."

"I'm not mad!" I say, wanting to scream but knowing I can't. "I'm just shocked. I don't know what to think. I don't have any right to be mad. You're both free, and adults, and to be perfectly honest, I don't even remember what Frank looks like."

Melanie assures me that he's still "really cute" and I start putting back on all the layers I'll need to protect myself from the cold. I pull a ten-dollar bill from my pocket and toss it on the table.

"It's on me," I say and Melanie says no, no, she's got a job, she'll pay, but I don't even answer, I just pull my hat down over my ears, try to smile, and say, "Well, Merry Christmas."

"I'm sorry, Ginger," she says. "About all those phone calls, I mean."

I look at her, sitting sadly under the chandelier, the light from the gumdrops illuminating the little tragedies of her life on her pale, tired face and I hate myself for not being more sophisticated, more urbane, for not being the kind of woman who would find the situation amusing, but I'm not, and even though I know in a week or two I will have forgotten all about it, that I'll go back to New York and tell Cassie about it and we'll sit at our favorite table at the Caffè Reggio and laugh and Melanie will call periodically and perhaps Frank will get on an extension phone and we'll all have a good chuckle about "old times" and I'll hang up the phone and wonder, "Why was I so upset?" Even though I know all that, it doesn't stop me from feeling as though my past is being polluted, revised, as if the mere fact of Melanie and Frank being together now somehow changes my own history, and I find that so terrifying I have to flee.

17

Peterson's has always been my favorite store in North Bay, the only department store, situated on a corner overlooking the main street in front and the river on the side. In the summer, during Boat Week, Mr. Peterson, Sr., would let us go up in his office and watch the yachts passing through the opened bridge and I would always wonder what would happen if a car was crossing the bridge just as the sides were raised. It has been a recurring nightmare of mine, being caught on a bridge as it opens, sliding back down, helpless, crashing into everything behind me. Its meaning is not particularly mysterious to me, it obviously has to do with my fear of being found out, that just as I thought I was well on my way to passing into another world, into another realm, out of my own past of mediocrity and dulled sensibility into a realm of beauty and meaning, I find myself helpless, cut off from the world I long to enter, destined to tumble back into insignificance.

I walk through the heavy doors and I am immediately engulfed in warmth and comfort. Everything in Peterson's is exactly the same as it has always been at Christmas: the huge white pillars are wrapped in red velvet ribbons and the old wooden display cases are hung with holly and ropes of pine. The mannequins stand where they have always stood, their hair painted in the same brown bob they've worn since before I was born, heedless of the hundreds of styles they've displayed over the years, always slightly out of date but never minding. When I was young, I was afraid of them, after having seen an episode of *The Twilight Zone* in which a mannequin thinks she's alive, or a human gets turned into a mannequin, or some such thing, I can't remember, all I remember is the terror it instilled in me: the terror of wanting to be something one is not and being forced to submit to reality.

I walk through the cosmetics section to the staircase leading down to the basement, where the office supplies are, next to the toys and the official Boy and Girl Scout outfitters. The little blond girl-mannequin is still standing at the bottom of the stairs, in her Girl Scout regalia, complete with green sash festooned with round badges of accomplishment, and I remember how diligently I would work to get those colorful little badges, before Virginia made me quit. I wanted them all, not because I cared about starting a fire or growing tomatoes or making an apron or grooming a horse or even being a good Girl Scout, but because I wanted my sash to have the most.

Cy Peterson—Mr. Peterson the Third to the younger set —finds me a typewriter without the annoying beeps and I lug it back to the car. On the way home, I stop at Wally's to buy some more comfort food and have a chat, but Wally isn't there. Instead, there's a sullen young man who doesn't know me and doesn't care, he's much more interested in watching

The Flintstones on his portable TV and that reminds me of Michael, another Flintstones freak. I don't get it, although, as a dinosaur myself, I ought to be able to identify. It's some kind of "guy thing," some kind of atavistic caveman thing, I suppose, but I find it rather pathetic. "Why don't you grow up?" I often ask Michael, but he doesn't want to, and why should he? Nobody else is.

Poppy's car is in the driveway, but Virginia's is gone. I go in the house and seek out Poppy, in his den, happily lost in the past.

"Where's Virginia?" I ask.

"She went to get the roast for tomorrow," he says. "She doesn't trust me."

I can't believe he let her take the car out, at night, in the snow, after she'd been drinking all day.

"Poppy, how could you let her drive?" I ask and he looks up, bewildered.

"What?" he asks. "What's wrong with that?"

"Poppy, she shouldn't be driving at all, much less in this weather, at night."

"Why not?" he asks. "She sees better than I do. She doesn't even wear glasses."

"She's been knocking back screwdrivers all day, that's why not," I say and he tells me not to worry, she took a nap, she's fine now.

Cease is in the living room, setting up the TV and the VCR. "Did you get the movie?" he yells and I say no, I didn't know he wanted me to get it.

"Dammit, Ginger," he screams, "it's probably gone by now," but I think that's unlikely, I'm pretty sure we're the only family in North Bay that has an annual tradition of watching *Psycho* on Christmas Eve.

Cease stomps into the den and stands in front of Poppy.

"I need your keys," he says and holds out his hand while Poppy fumbles in his pockets.

"They're on the kitchen table," I say and Cease glares at me and stomps out into the kitchen.

"All I can say is, it better be there," he shouts as he slams the door and Poppy and I look at each other.

"Well, well, well, Gingerbread girl," Poppy says. He looks around the room, searching for a topic of conversation, something we two could talk about. We really haven't had a conversation of any depth since the old days, when he used to ask me about Sputnik or whatever, and that was only because Virginia wasn't available.

"I got the typewriter," I say and he smiles.

"That's good," he says, "that's real good," and I think, This is my chance, this is my chance to really talk to Poppy, to get to know him, to discover what is underneath the silly jokes and hail-fellow-well-met bantering, to find out who he is.

"What are you going to do now?" he asks and I suggest we have a cup of coffee and talk, just the two of us.

"That would be real nice," he says and he pushes himself up from his chair with the grunt of the elderly and follows me into the kitchen.

"I'll skip the coffee," he says. "Too much caffeine is bad for the old ticker." He pats his chest lovingly. His old ticker has survived two heart attacks. "You-know-whats," Virginia calls them, fearing that to even mention the words would invite another, or, worse still, make Poppy feel old, even though that's precisely what he is.

I ask him what he'd like instead, as if I were the hostess and he the guest, but he doesn't even notice.

"Oh, water would be fine," he says, "if you don't mind."

I get him a glass of water and grab a can of pop from the refrigerator for myself and sit down at the table, opposite him in what used to be "my" place but which is now Virginia's, the rest of the table being crowded with ashtrays and the clean-air machine and crossword-puzzle dictionaries as well as Poppy's high school and college yearbooks, which he's searching through, digging out memories.

"Well, what would you like to talk about?" he asks and I don't know. How does one say to someone one has known all one's life, "I want to know who you are"? I know the outside; I can accurately predict how he will act in any given situation, but I haven't a clue as to what is going on inside. "Nothing," Virginia would say. "What you see is what you get," but of course that's impossible. Poppy couldn't possibly be as simple as he seems, so completely oblivious to the world around him.

He sits there, smiling expectantly, as if he were waiting for me to tell him a joke and I smile back, self-consciously, embarrassed, as if I were preparing myself to ask him to strip, which, in a sense, is exactly what I want him to do. Not physically, of course, I can't imagine anything more distasteful than seeing my seventy-six-year-old father naked, but, rather, emotionally. I want him to take off the glib, easygoing, glad-handing persona, to show me what is underneath, what it is he's successfully hidden all these years. I am tired of seeing the same old cheerful North Bay Booster, the Babbitt in Poppy. I want to see the rest.

"Have you ever considered just how much work goes into making your father the Nicest Man in North Bay?" Virginia once asked, and of course I hadn't, nor did I want to, for it wasn't only Virginia who had to do the work; in fact, she had abdicated pretty early on, leaving Cease and me to protect him, by keeping our little troubles to ourselves, hiding our pain or our sorrow or our humiliations, keeping them all a secret from Poppy. He never asked us to do this, but we all had the sense that we must keep everything unpleasant or ugly away from him, out of his view, keep him from knowing how unhappy we were, for if he knew, it would somehow blast the family to bits. The most important thing was making Poppy think we were happy, happy, happy, or if not happy at least "Okay." Virginia's breakdown, and her subsequent drunkenness, had been the most dangerous threat to our equilibrium, but we had somehow managed to get through even that without rocking our little lifeboat, we just plugged up the holes and baled out the bilgewater and pretended everything was fine, not, perhaps, as fine as before, but fine enough. India flew in and took responsibility for Virginia and we just rowed along, steady as she goes.

"Did you ever see India when you were in Paris?" I ask Poppy and he blinks, surprised by the question.

"You mean when I was in the service?" he asks, stalling for time. When else? Poppy has been all over the world, he likes to take a semiannual trip somewhere new, but he's running out of places to go, at least places where he'd want to go. Anywhere he hasn't been, he likes to say, isn't worth going to. But on all his travels and his many pilgrimages to Europe to traipse around gaping at cathedrals, he has never returned to Paris.

"Yes," I say and he scratches his head, as if the answer were hidden in his few wisps of white hair.

"I don't think so," he says. "It was a pretty busy time . . ."
I tell him he doesn't need to protect India, I know about her.

"What?" he asks. "What about India?"

"That she was a fraud," I say. "That she was never in the Resistance, that she never knew de Gaulle, that she never sabotaged anything other than herself."

"Oh," Poppy says. "I don't think she'd like to hear that."

"But did *you* know?" I ask. "Did you know what she was?"

"Who, me?" he says, grinning. "You know me—hear no

evil, speak no evil . . . Speaking of France, did I ever tell you about that place outside Versailles where the family had that mastiff?"

I nod. It's a cute story, a heartwarming story, a story about bravery and loyalty and love, a story about an old man, his daughter the beautiful war widow, and her young son, saved from the Nazis by Jacques the dog. The kind of story that would make a great Disney movie, the kind of story that is supposed to make me forget what I've asked him, make me forget about anything ugly or small. And Poppy tells it well, he remembers every detail down to the cracked heels of the woman's shoes, painted over with ink, and the little boy's fascination with cowboys and Buffalo Bill and the old man's metal tooth and the burrs clinging to the mastiff's ears. He takes you away, back with him to Rambouillet, and I can't help going, even though I want to stay right here, right in the kitchen, I want to stay here and find out what he knew and how he felt about it, I want to pull him back but it's too late, he's already on his way, he'll go from the mastiff in Rambouillet to the lap dog in Vienna and then he'll travel south, through Italy and then west to Spain and Portugal and the parrot in Lisbon, sailing across the ocean to the llama in Argentina and eventually he'll make his way back here, but not until either Virginia or Cease has returned and there's no longer a chance for intimacy.

I listen. I am tempted to walk over to the junk drawer and steal a pack of Virginia's cigarettes, to sink back into my own addiction, but I don't. As Poppy relives the highlights of his life for the umpteenth time, I think about how we are all rather stuck at the point in our lives where we seemed to be our best. Whatever we perceive to be the high point is where we want to stay, spending eternity as the prom queen or the football star, the war hero or the blue-ribbon pie baker. It's like watching a continuous slide show—Poppy tells us about his adventures as the pictures click up on the screen; then Virginia takes over and we view the scenes of her college life, when she was the star of the English Department. We see her in her cap and gown, looking fragile and beautiful, a porcelain figurine standing behind the podium addressing her fellow students and the faculty, talking about the importance of beauty in a world gone mad. Then Cease shows us his toys, clicking the slide changer to diagrams of voice boxes and motors, an endless succession of his favorite toys, dissected like laboratory animals. But when it comes to my turn, the screen goes blank. There is no high point in my life, and as I look into the glaring whiteness of the screen I am afraid there never will be one, that all my life will be just a blank, as if my slide had gotten stuck in the machine, chewed up, rejected.

I stand up. Poppy looks at me and asks if I'm all right, he tells me I look downright peaked, have I been eating enough vegetables?

I tell him I feel sick; it must have been that sundae I had at Penelope's.

"Well, you'd better go take a rest," he says. "We've got a big night ahead of us."

I nod and go upstairs, leaving Poppy alone with his llama, and shut myself in my bedroom. I lie on the bed and try to remember what my room was like when I lived here, before Virginia redecorated with roses and pale blues, covering up the memory of my bad taste, the bright orange flowered wallpaper that I chose when I was fourteen and in love with autumn. I wanted everything orange: orange wallpaper and orange furniture and orange frames around my mirror and the poster of Van Gogh's sunflowers. I wore only orange clothes—burnt orange and bright yellowish orange and reddish orange, even though it didn't become me, in fact, I couldn't have chosen a less becoming color but how I looked mattered less to me than how I felt and I wanted to feel like fall. "Don't blame me if everyone calls you a fruit," Virginia used to say as I'd head off to school in my orange ensemble, but I didn't care. Fall to me meant freedom, freedom and change. Every day, every minute, was a miracle, I'd walk to school with Maggie or Melanie and we'd marvel at the colors, the world seemed ready to explode with brightness and I wanted to feel that, to *be* that feeling, and so I surrounded myself with orange, orange, orange, much to Virginia's dismay.

"That god-awful color," she called it, trying to make me see it wasn't right for me, that it made me look sallow and unhealthy, like some kind of malnourished Appalachian waif, she said, and I suppose her hating it made it all the more appealing to me, it was something that could be mine alone, one of the few things in my life I wouldn't have to worry about being wrenched from my grasp during one of Virginia's frenzies, when she'd run through the house and gather together everything she thought she wanted, take it up to her bedroom and hide it in the closet so nobody could use it or see it or have it but her. Cease's toys, my books, Poppy's trophies and Good Citizen plaque would all disappear periodically; she'd hoard them away, in her closet, under her bed, in the drawers of her vanity, stealing everything we had that she wasn't a part of, everything except my orange things.

I look around the room and there is nothing orange in it now, except a tiny splash of it on the dress India is wearing in the portrait Virginia has placed on the wall, opposite my bed. It suddenly occurs to me that perhaps Virginia hated orange because India adored it, and perhaps part of my own love for it came from the same source.

I can't bear orange now, it hurts my eyes. I too prefer pastels. My apartment in New York is all pinks and blues and soft greys, and I wish I were there, lying on my hide-a-bed, staring out the window at the Roosevelt Island tram car gliding through the sky, over the rooftops and then out of view as it passes behind a new high-rise.

I have been watching that tram car pass back and forth for thirteen years now and I always promise myself that one day I'll get on it, one day I'll sail through the air and look at my apartment, from the outside in, see what my home looks like from another perspective. But I never do. When I'm walking down Second Avenue and I pass the entrance to the tram, I think, "One of these days . . ." but I suspect I never will get on it. I think I'm afraid, afraid to see how bleak and run-down my tenement looks from the sky, afraid that I won't be able to pick out my apartment, my home, my life, that it will be lost in the gloomy sameness of all the others.

I get up and look out my window, which faces the woods, bare now, and I am struck by how small the trees look. When we were young the woods seemed like a vast forest, but it's really only a scrubby little patch of sumac and birch, with a few maples sticking out. Of course the elms are all gone, and perhaps that's why it seems so paltry in comparison with my memory of it, perhaps it was indeed a vast forest, or at least a couple blocks' worth.

I think about Melanie, on the other side of the woods, and I feel childish and silly for having been so upset about her marrying Frank. Why shouldn't they marry each other? I certainly didn't want to marry him again, but I think I liked the idea of *his* never marrying again either, of my having been the one great love of his life, irreplaceable. It's humiliating to admit just how replaceable I've been; he's been married three or four times since our divorce, trying, I suppose, to get it right, which is completely in character for him. I, on the other hand, haven't even come close to marrying again, which I suppose is in character for me: knowing I will never get it right, I don't even bother to try.

18

"YO!" CEASE SHOUTS UP THE STAIRS. "G.M.! HURRY UP OR you'll miss the beginning."

Heaven forbid. By this time, we all know the movie by heart, we've been watching it every Christmas Eve since 1983 when Virginia made the mistake of asking, "Who's Norman Bates?" when Cease brought him up. "You've never seen *Psycho*?" Cease asked in disbelief and the rest is history, another tradition jammed in with all the others.

Michael loves it, loves the idea of us sitting in the living room watching *Psycho* together on Christmas Eve, while the carolers sing outside the front door, ignored and freezing, waiting for their Christmas cookies. He wanted to put it in his act but decided it was just too outrageous. "Who would believe that shit?" he asked and I shrugged; believe it or not, it's true, but I'd just as soon he didn't turn us into the Addams Family, North Bay style.

Virginia has made it back in one piece and everyone is assembled in the living room—a misnomer, since no one uses it anymore. It used to be the center of life in our house, a real place of living. It was where Cease and I would build our blanket forts behind the couch and where we'd have our birthday parties and where Poppy and Virginia would entertain their friends. It seemed there was always a party going on at our house back then, the room was filled with laughter, with the shrieks of happy children and the deep rumbling voices of adults. When Virginia was trying to be a Person, she'd have her women friends over for consciousness-raising groups, "men-are-shits parties," Poppy called them and Cease and I would hide in the playroom, waiting for all those nice ladies to use the S-word. But all that was B.V.B. After her breakdown, we all retreated to our own little worlds. Poppy moved into the guest room, Virginia claimed the den, Cease and I hid in our bedrooms or the playroom, and the living room became a kind of no-man's-land, silent and spooky, and the only person who ever entered it was me, and that was just to vacuum and dust.

I sit down on the couch and Cease flicks on the remote control. The FBI warning appears on the TV screen and we all watch it, transfixed. The music begins, but instead of Bernard Herrmann's frenetic strings pulsing the credits forward, Mickey Mouse appears in his sorcerer's hat.

"What is this shit?" Cease asks, as Jiminy Cricket begins singing "When You Wish Upon a Star."

Virginia begins to laugh. "You got the wrong movie, dear," she says and Cease pounds the fast-forward button, zooming through Geppetto's dance through his workshop with Pinocchio and Figaro.

"I didn't get the wrong movie," he says, "that stupid jerk at the video store *gave* me the wrong movie. I'll kill him!"

"Now, now," Poppy says, "I'm sure it wasn't his fault. Somebody probably returned the movie in the wrong box . . ."

"I don't give a shit!" Cease shouts. "It's his job to make sure the right movie is in the right box! Now what are we gonna do, it's too late to go back!"

"Thank God for small favors," Virginia says. "I'm sick of that movie. Everybody always blames the mother, but after all, it was the son who was the wacko."

"Yeah, but who made him a wacko?" Cease asks. "The mother."

"We don't know that," Virginia says. "We only have his word for it, and he's a fruitcake."

"You're missing the whole point of the movie," Cease says. "He's a fruitcake *because* of the mother, she was so clinging and demanding and awful he *had* to murder her, and then he had to become her."

"Says who?" Virginia asks. "We don't even get the mother's side of the story. She's a corpse, all we know is that he killed her when she got a new husband. He was just jealous, jealous and crazy, and she was probably a very nice person."

"Yeah, well, what about all that screaming and nagging and name-calling Norman does when he's his mother, he didn't just make that up . . ."

"How do you know?" Virginia asks. "He's probably insane with guilt so he has to come up with some reason to hate her, and since there probably wasn't one, because she was probably a very nice person who really *wouldn't* 'harm a fly,' he makes up that cock-and-bull harpy he keeps down in the fruit cellar."

" 'Cock-and-bull harpy,' " Cease mutters and Poppy says, "How about a game of Monopoly?"

"Ugh," we all say and Poppy gets up from his chair and

stretches. "Well," he says, "in that case I guess I'll go up and wait for Santa." He chuckles and heads up the stairs.

I suppose there is something to be said for even the most ridiculous tradition. If nothing else, they keep the time filled and now here we are, Virginia, Cease, and myself, sitting together in no-man's-land like warring parties at the negotiation table. It's dangerous—Cease is more furious than usual because he didn't get to see *Psycho*; Virginia is no longer down in the muck of self-pity, but she's not out of the abyss, she's only resting on a ledge and anything could toss her back in. And me? I'm just terrified. There's something in the air, something ominous, but I can't get a sense of what it is. All I know is that my instincts have got me in the Alert Stage— tense, watchful, protected.

"I think I'll go up, too," Virginia says, gathering together her necessities—drink, cigarettes, and large-print thriller— and I am somewhat relieved, at least we will make it through tonight without another battle.

"Merry Christmas," she says as she starts up the stairs and Cease says, "Yeah, and ho ho ho to you, too."

When her door closes I turn to Cease. "Why are you so mean to her?" I ask him. "Why don't you just give it up? She isn't going to change, you know, so why do you torment her like that?"

"I can't help myself," Cease says. He begins taking the remote control apart, fiddling with the insides. "I wonder if I could make some kind of stink bomb with this?" he says. "Flick on *Wheel of Fortune* and poof! Eau de dog-do."

"She's an old woman," I say. "She feels horrible about what happened, she's wasted her whole life drinking away her guilt, why don't you just leave her alone?"

"Look," he says, "let's not talk about it, okay?"

"No, not okay," I say. "I want to know why you can't just give the poor woman some peace. She wasn't *always* a crappy mother, you know. At least she didn't go nuts until after we had our crucial nurturing, and even afterwards she wasn't all *that* bad, she was about a five on the Crappy Mother scale, it could have been worse."

"'Crucial nurturing,'" Cease sneers. "You sound like some phony-baloney shrink. What do you know about it?"

"Enough to know she wasn't a monster. For Christ's sake, why do you act as if she was?"

"I said I don't want to talk about it," he says, but *I* do. I don't know why all of a sudden I feel I have to be Virginia's defender, unless perhaps it's just a matter of fairness. Cease has tormented her for over twenty years, much longer than she tormented him, and it seems to me it's time to call it a draw.

"Will you put that thing down and talk to me?" I ask, but he just keeps right on fiddling, ignoring me, just as he used to ignore Virginia, pretending to be in another world while she screamed at him for some childish misdemeanor, leaving out the milk or something, leaving his muddy boots in the hall where she could have tripped over them, as if she needed an obstacle to make her crash flat on her face.

He gets up and goes into the kitchen for the toolbox. I follow him, nagging, prodding—dangerous behavior with Cease, but I'm determined to get some kind of response from him. Why? I don't know, I guess that's the form my own madness takes, I have to know *why* he won't just let it go.

"Get off my back, Ginger," he says as he rummages around in the toolbox, pulling out a tiny screwdriver and smiling.

"Cease, you're not a little boy anymore, you're a grown man."

He glares at me. "Will you just get off it?" he says. "How I feel is my own business. Why don't you stop harping about *my* anger and do something about your own?"

I don't know what he's talking about; I'm not angry, not anymore.

"I dealt with that," I say and he grunts.

"I *did*," I insist.

"Yeah, right," he says, slamming the toolbox shut. "This from the woman who used to run around screaming, 'She's a *vampire*! She's trying to suck the life out of me!'"

"That was a long time ago," I say. "I told you, I've dealt with it."

"Oh yeah," he says. "I'm okay, you're okay, and all that bullshit."

I sigh. "It's a little more complex than that," I say and he scowls at me.

"You are so condescending," he says. "Will you just leave me alone?"

"All right," I say, offended by his remark but letting it slide. This is, after all, not about me, it's about him, about him and Virginia. "I promise I won't say one more word about letting it go if you'll just tell me *why*. Why do you keep tormenting her like that?"

He looks at me, his eyes a hard light grey, like the toolbox, cold and without feeling.

"You want to know *why*?" he asks. "You really want to know, Freudella? You're such an expert on human nature, Miss I'll-Live-Anyone's-Life-But-My-Own. How come you can't figure it out yourself?"

"Well, I think . . ."

"You *think*. That's about all you do, you think this and you think that, but you don't *know* shit."

"Wait a minute," I say. "Why are you attacking *me*?"

"Because you won't get off my back," he says, pointing the screwdriver at me like a dagger and I suddenly go on Red Alert, I realize I have overstepped my bounds, wandered into

the minefield of Cease's fury and there is no place I can run
for cover.

"You want to know *why*?" he says and now I don't but it's
too late, he's going to tell me something I don't want to hear,
and I fight the urge to clasp my hands over my ears and run
upstairs screaming. A fluttering newsreel of horror flickers
about in my brain—a dungeon of childhood tortures, with
Cease cowering in a dank corner while Virginia, with a
black executioner's hood over her head, slowly approaches,
cackling . . .

"You think *she* made me what I am," he says, "and I let
everybody think that. I let *her* think that, but the truth is, I
made *her*. I made *her* into what she is."

"What are you talking about?" I ask, the vision evaporat-
ing, to my great relief. It's just more of Cease's nonsense.

"You don't blame yourself for her breakdown, do you?" I
ask and he laughs, in that hard brittle cackle of Virginia's.

"Spare me the Alateen number," he says. "The you're-not-
responsible shit. I *am* responsible."

"Cease . . ." I say, going toward him, but he holds out the
screwdriver like a clump of garlic and I back off.

"Why did she have a breakdown?" Cease asks.

"Because she thought she killed Roger," I say.

"Right," Cease says. "The Dead Brother. And what really
killed him?"

"The Lego piece," I say.

"You still don't get it, do you?" he says. "You're so stupid,
you're *all* so stupid."

"What are you talking about?" I ask again and he starts
pacing madly around the kitchen, viciously pounding the
counter with each step.

"Didn't you ever wonder how he *got* it? What do you
think, he pole-vaulted out of his crib, crawled downstairs,

grabbed a Lego piece out of the playroom, crawled back upstairs, and ate it?"

"Oh my God," I say.

"Bingo!" Cease cries. "Dr. Moore wins the jackpot!"

"Oh my God," I say.

I don't know what to do. Cease is standing across the room, his face as grey as his eyes, grey and cracked, like old cement, and I am afraid he is going to disintegrate. I want to go to him, hold him together, but I am afraid if I touch him he will slide through my arms, crumble into dust at my feet.

"Oh my God," I say again and he glares at me.

"What are you, a broken record?" he says. "I heard you the first time."

"You've lived with that all these years?" I ask. "Why didn't you say anything?"

"Say what? 'No sweat, Mom, you didn't kill him, I did'?"

"But Cease, nobody *killed* him. It wasn't as if you intentionally set out to murder him."

He turns away from me. "How do *you* know?" he asks. "How do you know what I set out to do?"

I suddenly have a vision of Cease sitting alone in his trailer, endlessly brooding about Roger—"Did I or didn't I?"—burying himself deeper and deeper in doubt and guilt and despair, becoming more furious with each inch he descends, blaming himself, blaming Virginia. It would drive anyone insane and it's a wonder he's not worse than he is.

"Good God, Cease," I say. "You were a *child.*"

He is standing in the corner where the cupboards meet the stove and he slowly collapses, his back sliding down the smooth oak cabinet, his shirt catching on the brass knob, and he begins to sob—loud, gasping, asthmatic heaves.

"He wanted to play with it," he wails. "How was I supposed to know he'd try to *eat* it?" and I run across the room and take him in my arms, cradling him like a child. To my surprise, he doesn't push me away, nor does he cling to me, he just sits there, limp and heavy, crying while I rock him.

"I couldn't tell," he says. "I was too afraid. I was afraid they'd send me to The Home, afraid they'd lock me up forever and everyone would hate me."

"Oh, Cease," I say and he looks at me, surprised I'm there, surprised he's in my arms, but still he doesn't push me away.

"I let her think she did it. In a way, I killed them both."

"Cease, you didn't kill anybody. It was an accident," I say but he doesn't hear me.

"What's that line in *Psycho*?" he asks—"'Matricide is probably the most unbearable crime of all, most unbearable to the son who commits it.'"

I don't know what to do. I feel utterly inadequate to cope with his pain, his guilt, but I can't just leave him sitting down here in the kitchen like a collapsed marionette. I don't know how to reach him; I don't even know if he's reachable anymore.

"Come on," I say, trying to lift him up. "I'll help you upstairs."

He scowls at me. "I don't need your help," he says, but he does, he's caught on the knob, and I unfasten him.

"Humor me," I say, "I have to feel like I'm *doing* something," and he gives in, leaning on me as we slowly ascend the stairs. With some difficulty, I get him to his bed, and he falls in it, face up, staring at the ceiling. I take off his shoes and turn out the light.

"Ginger," he says, "are you going to tell?"

He looks just like a little boy, the little boy he once was. He was my best friend, before Roger died, before he cut himself off from the world, before his sweet, silly humor turned rough and vicious, before he started to punish himself and everyone else who came too close to him.

"I think *you* should," I say and he shudders.

"Are you going to tell?" he asks again and I tell him to try to get some sleep. I mimic Poppy—"We've got a big day ahead of us, Ceaseless," I say in a deep voice, but he doesn't laugh, he doesn't even smile.

19

I CAN'T SLEEP. ALL I CAN THINK ABOUT IS POOR CEASE IN that run-down trailer out in the Oregon woods, eating himself alive with guilt and hatred. *Frankenstein.* It always comes back to *Frankenstein,* but in this case it isn't quite clear who created whom, who is the Creator and who the Monster. They both think they "made" the other. Virginia thinks her drinking and negligence turned Cease into a mean, sullen lout; Cease thinks he turned Virginia into a drunken shrew; and so they endlessly chase each other over the ice, around and around the Pole, trying to destroy each other.

Now Cease's life makes sense, all of it makes sense, and I want to cry out in rage for the wastefulness of it, the stupidity of it. I think about the boy he was, before Roger's death: happy, active, "full of beans," as Virginia used to say, hilariously funny, keeping us endlessly entertained with his imitations of his teachers, of all the neighbors, putting on little comedies with his toys. "The Madhouse," Virginia called our home, never dreaming how prescient she was. There were always herds of whooping boys running up and down the stairs and out the porch, shaking the house with their joy at just being alive. I hated them, of course, they were, after all, just yucky boys, disturbing my friends and me while we played jacks on the tiled bathroom floor, rushing in and farting just as I was about to "go around the world," but I missed them after Cease retreated into his own world, I missed their noise, their foolishness, their exuberance.

"Freud calls guilt a useless emotion," Greta always used to say, but useless or not it's still deadly. "You're trying to make me feel guilty," Michael often says when I take him to task for some misdemeanor, forgetting my birthday or not showing up at my reading, but that's the last thing I want to do. I've seen what guilt can do; consciously or unconsciously, you begin to despise the source of it, you want it to go away, to leave you alone, to disappear. Who wants to be reminded of what a shit she is? And so we flee, or if we're like Cease, we turn it around, turn the one we've hurt into some sort of evil demon we must crush at every opportunity. And if we're like Virginia, we rant.

I think about Virginia's letter. The "Savior" letter, I call it. She must have written it years ago, when we were still trying to get her into a rehab, when Poppy was determined to save her from herself. She had never finished it; she just folded it up and placed it in my dresser drawer, obviously leaving it there for me to find. I didn't want to read it; I knew I would be sorry if I did, but I couldn't help myself. It's still there and I drag myself out of bed and get it.

"We hate the one who saves us," she wrote. "The Good Samaritan, trudging down into the oblivion in his Wellington boots, squishing through the mire like a fisherman, searching us out and pleading, 'Please come back, please come back,' trying to convince us he's doing it for us, but he's doing it for himself. 'I am here because I want to be here,' I hiss, hiding behind a bush filled with inch-long spikes, but he snaps his reel and hooks me, drags me out through the thorns, 'for your own good, for your own good,' he chants as he reels me in, bloody and furious . . .'"

That was as far as she got, but that was far enough for me. It had never occurred to me that there were those who didn't want to be saved, to whom the guilt of an endless gratitude would be unbearable, worse than whatever it was they were suffering in the first place.

I hear a loud thump from Virginia's room and then the sound of Poppy's slippered feet padding down the hall. I hear his voice murmuring in her room and I wonder what's going on. There's no sound or broken glass, no wails from Virginia, so it's doubtful she's having one of her fits.

"Ginny," Poppy says, "what are you doing down there?"

There's no answer from Virginia and Poppy's voice rises. "Ginny, why don't you get up? Ginny, what are you doing down there, get up!"

I grab my bathrobe and run to her room. Virginia is lying by the side of the bed, looking up at Poppy in wonder.

"Poppy, what's wrong?" I ask and he turns to me, dazed.

"She won't get up," he says.

I kneel down beside her. "Virginia, are you all right?" I ask but she just stares at me, as if wondering what I'm doing there, wondering what we're both doing there.

"Poppy, we'd better call an ambulance," I say and his eyes fill with tears.

"She just needs to get back to bed," he says, and leans over, trying to pull her up. "Come on, Ginny, you don't want to sleep down here."

I reach for the phone and dial 911. My hands are shaking,

my blood burns with a hot rush of terror, "My mother," I tell the operator. "Hurry, there's something wrong with my mother."

She wants to know what's wrong, is it a heart attack, and I try not to scream at her. "I don't know what it is," I say, as Poppy starts to cry. "She's on the floor. She's not moving!"

"Please get up," Poppy is pleading. "Ginny, get up and go to bed."

I give the operator our address and hang up. Cease appears wraith-like in the doorway, looking somewhat confused, as if we were acting out charades and he didn't get it.

"Go get dressed," I tell Poppy, trying to pull him up, "the ambulance is coming," but he won't budge, he just kneels over Virginia, crying softly, begging her to get up.

"Get Poppy's coat," I tell Cease, "and unlock the front door while you're downstairs."

He silently disappears down the stairs. "You are so controlling," a voice says—Michael's, one of the Judges', Cease's, I don't know. I shake it out of my head. "Don't bug me now," I say and Poppy looks up at me, furious, thinking that I am criticizing Virginia for inconveniencing me. I don't explain, how can I explain? I just lean over Virginia, pat her cheek, and tell her everything is going to be okay. She smiles and tears ooze out of the corners of her eyes. She's so white. I think she should be grey; there should be a bluish tinge to her skin, there should be a darkening shadow, but she is absolutely, purely white and I wonder if all those dark images of death are simply wrong, if death is, in reality, white.

"Don't die," I plead, silently, for I know I can't say the word "die" in front of Poppy. He'd collapse too and I would be an orphan, instantly.

The ambulance arrives and the medics run upstairs. They gently pry Poppy away and Cease wraps him up in his coat.

"I'll go with Poppy in the ambulance," Cease says as the

medics attach a plastic mask to Virginia's face. "You take the car and meet us there."

I nod. The medics take Virginia downstairs and Poppy follows like a lost puppy. Cease guides him and I am overwhelmed with tenderness for them all, I want Virginia to be all right, I want Virginia to be all right and Poppy to be happy and Cease to be at peace with himself. I suddenly realize it's Christmas and although I am not a believer, I pray. "Please, dear God, let everything be okay," I say and run to my room to get dressed.

20

VIRGINIA IS IN INTENSIVE CARE. POPPY AND CEASE ARE SIT-
ting in the waiting room, in their coats and identical pajamas.
Black Watch plaid flannel. I am surprised I didn't notice this
before; I am rather obsessive about details, the seemingly
trivial minutiae of life. In my work, any trifle, even a pair of
pajamas, can turn out to be the key that unlocks the door behind which lies the secret of a life.

We have the waiting room to ourselves. I sit down on an
orange vinyl-coated bench, next to Cease.

"How is she?" I ask and he shrugs.

Poppy is trying hard not to cry, to be the strong father, but
his bloodshot, teary eyes betray his fear.

"Have you seen the doctor?" I ask and he shakes his head.

"The nurse said they'd come and get us," he says, looking
hopefully toward the door, but there is no one there.

I get up and walk to the window. This is the new wing overlooking Edison Park and the river, built after I left North Bay. Everything is dark, except the arc of lights on the bridge to Canada, sparkling like a low-lying constellation in the otherwise starless sky. I wonder if it will snow.

I feel nothing. No fear, no pain, no sorrow, no fatigue. I think I should be feeling *something,* but I'm not. It's as if I'm in some kind of bland limbo—not shock, I don't think, although never having experienced it before, I don't exactly know what "being in shock" feels like.

I sometimes think I am stuck in a kind of eternal adolescence, in which I think there is a specific, appropriate way to feel for every occasion, and since I don't know what that is, I shut down entirely. This isn't uncommon, of course, but I ought to know better. I *do* know better, but that doesn't stop me from suspecting there is some kind of secret guidebook in which all the answers are given, a kind of behavioral Bible, to which everyone has access but me.

"Mr. Moore?" a voice asks and we all turn toward the door, where a nurse is standing.

"You can see her now," he says, and Poppy jumps up and grabs his hand.

"Is she all right?" he begs.

"She's conscious," he says, noncommittally, but that's good enough for Poppy, and he tears off down the hall. We follow after him, catching up when he is stopped by an automatic door that won't open. He pushes and pulls and jumps up and down on the floor, and Cease and I can't help it, we laugh, softly, guiltily; it's not funny but it is.

"Here," the nurse says, pushing a metal square attached to the wall. The doors swing open with a loud swoosh and Poppy wobbles through them and I watch, from behind, watch him growing older with each step, staggering down the corridor like a drunk, hunched over and unsteady, an old,

old man. I look at the nurse, who is also watching him, but with a clinical eye. "Osteoporosis," he is probably thinking, "ataxia," and I want to scream, I want time to stop, or at least slow down, I want Virginia to live and I want Poppy to stand up straight, I want Cease to forgive himself and I want to feel again.

"'I want, I want, I want.'" The man's chiding voice still haunts me after all these years, I can hear it in my head as clearly as if he were standing next to me. I have no idea who he is, was, just a man at an Al-Anon meeting I attended years ago, when both Melanie and Virginia were tormenting me with their drunken phone calls. I rarely spoke at those meetings, I would just sit there and listen, waiting to feel relieved, but I never did. One night, after a particularly vicious conversation with Virginia, I dragged myself to a meeting and raised my hand and began jabbering. I have no idea what I said, I just needed to "vent," as they say, and after I had finished, the man raised his hand and nodded his head at me and said, "I used to be like that." He scowled and mimicked me in a horrid, whining voice: "I want, I want, I want." I don't remember anything else he said, just that high-pitched, grating, humiliating whine: "I want, I want, I want." I was so mortified I tried to run from the meeting but several well-meaning, kindly women stopped me, saying, "Don't mind him, he's just a kook," but it was too late, that voice, those words, were embedded in my mind forever, chiding me for my greed, my insatiable need, my selfishness. I vowed never to want again. With the help of the Panel of Judges and that man's voice, I squashed down every desire as it bubbled up inside, and while it was difficult at first, eventually it worked, eventually I wanted nothing, but instead of giving me peace it gave me—nothing.

And now I realize, too late, always too late, that wanting is wonderful, desire is what life is all about, not in a material, grasping sense, although I suppose that works when all else fails, not in the sense of wanting in order to have, but in the sense of a passionate desire to be alive, to want to give one's life a sense of purpose, to want to be a part of the world, a part of something greater than oneself.

Poppy has stopped. He is standing in front of a large glass window, talking to a white-coated man, the doctor, I suppose, glancing anxiously through the window and tottering dangerously. The doctor takes Poppy's arm and leads him inside the room.

"Are we all allowed to go in?" I ask the nurse and he nods and leaves us standing outside the window. Poppy is hunched over Virginia, holding her hand and weeping. Her eyes are open but unfocused, she is staring straight ahead, angrily, it seems to me, but she is heavily sedated, barely conscious, how can she be angry? There are numerous tubes extending from her body, tiny clear IV tubes and a huge blue plastic tube the size of a vacuum-cleaner hose coming out of her neck. The machines are beeping and whirring and chugging and I feel as if I've suddenly been transported to some bizarre science-fiction writer's nightmare. I know that all these tubes and machines are the pride of modern science, the machinery of life and hope, but they seem ugly and evil and terrifying to me.

Cease and I enter the room. "Ginny," Poppy is saying, clutching her hand, "can you hear me? Are you going to be all right?" His desperation is palpable and I turn away. I can't bear to watch him, to watch them, it seems almost obscene, as if I were spying on an act of the most excruciating intimacy.

I turn to the doctor, and ask him how she is. He seems relieved to have an excuse to leave the room and he ushers me out in the hall. Cease follows, and we stand in the corridor, pretending to listen to the doctor, pretending to understand what he is saying, but it's all gibberish. I hear the words but they make no sense: congestive heart failure, emphysema, ventilator, bypass, renal something or other. All I want to know is whether she will live, and he's trying to tell me, but I don't understand.

He tells us we should take Poppy and go home, she's out of danger for the time being and we all need some rest. He gives me his card and tells me to call his office to set up an appointment; he wants to talk to us, but he doesn't say about what.

"I can't get him out of there," I say, shaking my head toward Poppy, who is almost lying in the bed with Virginia, and the doctor nods and goes to get him. Cease and I walk down the hall to avoid witnessing the scene.

"How come he gave *you* his card?" Cease asks when we get to the nurse's station.

"What card?" I ask. "What are you talking about?"

"The doctor," he says. "How come he gave *you* the card? I'm the oldest."

"Well, maybe I look older than you," I say but that's not good enough.

"He never even looked at me," he says. "He addressed everything to you. I'm the oldest. I'm the man. He should have been talking to *me*."

"What difference does it make who he was looking at?" I ask. "Maybe he was looking at me because I'm fully dressed and you're in your pajamas. I don't know why he was looking at me, maybe he thinks I'm cute."

Cease snorts. "Fat chance," he says and leans against the wall.

I wonder if Cease is going to transfer his hatred of Virginia onto me, if knowing his secret is enough to make him hate me.

"Let's not fight," I say, stupidly—to Cease being quarrelsome isn't "fighting," it's his way of being, his way of moving through the world, arms flailing, eyes flashing, mouth snarling, and asking him to be anything else is absurd.

"I'm not fighting," he says. "I just want to know who put you in charge."

Poppy is coming down the hall, leaning against the nurse, weeping.

"Look, Cease," I say, "I don't want to be in charge of anything. Let's just get Poppy home."

He grunts and we each take one of Poppy's arms and slowly make our way to the elevator.

21

POPPY IS IN THE DEN, TOSSING VIRGINIA'S CHRISTMAS
presents into a big black garbage bag.

"Do you think we should take the typewriter?" he asks
when he notices me standing in the doorway.

I shake my head. I don't think we should take any of
the presents, but Poppy insists. "It's Christmas," he says, "her
feelings would be hurt if she didn't get any gifts."

He picks up each package, reads the name on the
To–From tag, and then either throws it in the bag or in a pile
next to the withering tree.

"What about ours?" he asks, picking up a large box
wrapped in gold, raising it to his ear and shaking it. "Do you
think we should take them to the hospital and open them
there?"

"No," I say, and Poppy wants to know when I turned into such a Scrooge.

"I just don't think it's appropriate, under the circumstances," I say but Poppy thinks there couldn't be anything *more* appropriate than giving gifts on Christmas.

"Do you think we should get something for the nurses?" he asks. "Maybe we should take them one of these cheese things."

I shrug. It doesn't matter what I think; he's not asking me for my opinion, he's just voicing his ideas, as they occur to him, in the form of a question.

"And we've got those chocolates, too," he says, "the ones Bob Meyers sent. We haven't opened them yet."

He begins wandering around the house, looking for things to give away, little bribes to keep Virginia alive. He would give away everything if he thought it would help, he would give away everything of his own and everything of ours as well, but he'll start small, with the chocolates and the "cheese things," and work his way up from there.

The doorbell rings and I flee upstairs; it will be another neighbor with a casserole and concern, and while I am grateful for their kindness, I can't bear to watch as Poppy tells his story, over and over again, falling apart afresh, growing more ancient with each telling. When they leave he will be furious with me, with my seeming rudeness, but how can I tell him I am fleeing not from them but from him?

He's been on the phone to the hospital four times already this morning and it's only nine o'clock. Virginia is being moved out of Intensive Care but we can't see her until eleven, an eternity for Poppy. "Is she all right?" he keeps asking the nurses, "is she going to be okay?" but all they'll say is that she's being moved. "That's a good sign, isn't it?" he asked hopefully when he got off the phone, and Cease said, "It beats being moved to the morgue," but fortunately Poppy didn't hear him.

I think about calling Cassie, calling someone in New York, someone who can remind me of the person I am there. It's been less than a week since I left but it seems like decades, it seems as though I have slipped inextricably back into the person I was here, the person I hate being. I feel completely powerless, a being with no will, no say, no substance, a dead leaf sucked along in Poppy's wake.

I think, even, of calling Michael, but that would be insane. I know better than to mention to him the dirtiest of the four-letter words—"need"—he'd turn on me, throw it back in my face, call me "needy" and flee and I couldn't bear that right now. I don't take it well under the best of circumstances, but now it would be as deadly as putting a gun to my head.

The front door closes and Poppy calls up the stairs. "Come on, you two," he shouts. "Let's get going."

Cease is driving Poppy in Virginia's car; I'm going to take my own. I want to be able to leave if I need to, and when Poppy wants to know why we can't all go together—after all, it's Christmas—I tell him I have to come home early to put the roast in the oven.

It's gorgeous outside, gorgeous but dangerous. We must have had rain or sleet overnight, the trees are covered with a delicate crystal coating of ice, dazzling in the sunlight. The roads are awful, but fortunately the hospital is close and we inch our way there in a sliding convoy.

Before I even get out of my car, Poppy is sliding across the parking lot with the bag of presents and I am afraid he will fall and hurt himself, but miraculously he makes it and stands in the lobby, impatiently waiting for us. We take the elevator to the fourth floor and as soon as the door opens, he's gone, zooming down the hall, dragging the garbage bag behind him. He refuses to let either Cease or me carry it—being Santa is his job, and he won't delegate even the schlepping to either of us elves.

"He looks like a bag guy," Cease comments as Poppy disappears around a corner, and it's true, his camel-hair coat is filthy, the lining peeps out under the hem in the back, the wool cap I gave him for Christmas last year is smushed and dirty. "*You* try to get it away from him," Virginia said when I suggested a little dry cleaning wouldn't hurt. "He thinks that coat is some kind of holy relic, he won't give it up till it's eighty degrees."

When we round the corner he has disappeared. I feel a jolt of panic, even though I know he's probably just found Virginia and he's already in her room, piling presents on her bed. It is astonishing to me how many disasters my mind can present to me in the space of a few seconds, in less time than it takes to say, "What room is Virginia Moore in?" it can show me any number of horrors: Poppy being placed on a gurney and rushed back downstairs to the Emergency Room; Virginia lying dead in her bed with Poppy collapsed over her, stricken with a heart attack of his own; Poppy lost and wandering around the hospital with his garbage bag, being tossed out like a bum by the security guards.

When we get to Virginia's room he is already there, standing next to her and beaming like a thrilled child, dripping tears on her hand while she looks up at him helplessly. The tubes are all still attached to her and I notice there are restraints on her wrists as well. I don't want to think about why they are there.

"Maybe we should let them be alone for a while," I suggest to Cease and he shrugs and leans against the wall. He looks fairly baglike himself. I have always thought that slovenliness came from a sense of self-hatred, that it was connected to depression and self-loathing, and while that could very well be true for Cease, it doesn't explain Poppy, who is the only person in our family who even comes close to cheerful. "He just doesn't care," Virginia always says, "he doesn't notice the dirt." Which, considering Virginia's distaste for cleaning, is a good thing. One Christmas she gave me a sampler, stitched out by her own numb fingers, which read: DULL WOMEN HAVE IMMACULATE HOMES. I never knew whether she meant to acknowledge me as the true slob I am or to insult me for all those years of obsessive cleaning, and of course I didn't ask. Not that it matters, it's a good joke in either case and everyone who enters my apartment points to it and laughs, even though we all know one doesn't need to be spotless to be dull.

Poppy sticks his head out the door. "Come on," he tells us, "let's have Christmas."

We follow him into Virginia's room. Fortunately, there is no one in the other bed and Poppy has piled Virginia's presents on it.

"There's one we didn't bring," he tells her, "but it's something you wanted."

I walk over to the side of the bed and stand there, looking down at her. "How do you feel?" I ask and she closes her eyes wearily. It's a stupid question, she obviously feels horrible, but I don't know what else to say. She is all puffy and bloated, as if one of the tubes were pumping air into her, pumping her up like a balloon, and I am afraid she will burst. Her face is grey and taut; her arms are covered with blue and yellow bruises, but worst of all are the restraints, little white strips of cloth tied around her wrists and then again around the bed frame. She lifts up her hand helplessly and stares at me, pleadingly I think, asking me with her eyes why she has to endure this humiliation.

Poppy hasn't seemed to notice the restraints, he thrusts a

gaily wrapped box at her and then drops it on her stomach. She winces and tries to laugh.

I take it and begin to unwrap it.

"That's not for you!" Poppy cries and I say I know it's not, Virginia can't open it herself.

"Why not?" he says, "she's not a cripple," and she raises her other hand and pulls the restraint tight, tugging on it with her wrist.

Poppy is horrified. "What are they doing to you?" he asks, untying the restraint. "What kind of place is this?"

A nurse enters, smiling. "Merry Christmas," she says and Poppy begins to shout at her.

"Why is she tied up?" he demands. "What are you people doing to her?"

The nurse scowls. "Just a precaution," she says coldly, "so she won't hurt herself."

"Hurt herself?" Poppy shouts. "Why would she do something like that?"

The nurse shrugs and waves us all out of her way. "You'll have to leave the room for a minute," she says, wrapping a blood-pressure band around Virginia's arm, and Cease takes Poppy by the elbow and guides him from the room.

Poppy is bewildered and terrified and furious, he doesn't know what's going on, for once in his life he's not in control and he doesn't know what to do so he rages. He wobbles down to the nurses' station, demanding to speak to a doctor, to someone who's in charge, and while I sympathize with the nurses I also sympathize with him. I remember seeing a movie once, a movie about doctors, I suppose, in which a man is admitted to an Emergency Room by his wife, who follows the doctors around, screaming hysterically, demanding to know what is wrong. She's in the way, she's a bother, a real class-A pain in the ass. The scene is shot to make the viewer identify with the overworked resident, to make one want to shout, "Shut up, you idiot, and let him do his job!" and yet now that I'm cast in the role of the idiot myself, now that Poppy and Cease and I are all idiots, I too want to run through the halls, screaming hysterically, trying to find someone who will tell me what's wrong, why she's being restrained, what those horrid machines are doing to her, what it all *means.*

Poppy's bribe didn't work; the nurses are too busy to talk to him, it's Christmas, they're short-staffed, the doctor is home with his family, he'll have to wait till tomorrow. Visiting hours are almost over and Virginia hasn't opened her presents yet. He stoops lower and lower with each defeat and whatever is left of my heart is breaking, I can't bear to watch this.

"Cease," I say, "can't you stop him?"

He looks at me. "Are you serious?" he asks.

"Can't you try?" I beg.

"What's the matter with you?" he asks. "You're the control freak in the family, why don't you get him to stop?"

"Cease, please," I beg and he sighs and walks over to Poppy.

"Let's go get some coffee," he says and, amazingly, Poppy stops in the middle of his harangue and follows Cease obediently to the elevator. Poppy has always been big on keeping oneself occupied, and I suppose in his helplessness he feels he must do something—whether it's ranting at the nurses or drinking coffee with Cease makes little difference, just as long as there is something in his head that will crowd out the thought of death.

The nurse who banished us calls to me from the doorway of Virginia's room. "Okay," she says, kind now, "you can come in."

Virginia is sitting up, or rather, the nurse has adjusted the bed so that she is in an upright position. Her eyes are closed and I enter quietly.

"Virginia?" I say and her eyes open.

I walk over to her side and take her hand. It is cold and gnarled and limp. I squeeze it, gently, and she glares at me.

I tell her Poppy and Cease are down in the cafeteria, having coffee. "They'll be right back," I say and she rolls her eyes.

I can't think of anything to say. I suppose I should be making my peace with her, isn't that what one is supposed to do when one's parent is dying, but I don't see the point in assailing her with all her flaws and then benevolently forgiving her, nor in battering myself with my own and asking her forgiveness. I would like to tell her I love her, but I can't. The words just won't come. I do love her, I *do,* but I just can't say it and I hate myself for that, for not being able to give her that, such a tiny little thing, just a few words, what difference does it make if they sound flat and false, even though they're *not* false? I feel trapped, pushed into a corner, forced to do something that is so totally against my nature it seems criminal.

I squeeze her hand, harder, hoping that I can convey by touch what I cannot say, what I fear would annihilate us both. If I say it, she will die and I will shatter because that's the way our love is, not gentle and soft but overpowering, absolute, terrifying.

Where are Poppy and Cease? I want to flee, to run away, to go home and crawl into one of my childhood hiding places—the attic, my playhouse, the shrubs at the beach.

Virginia wriggles her hand away from me. She is motioning toward the machines, weakly waving her fingers at them.

"What?" I ask. "Do you need something?"

She shakes her head furiously and continues waving her hand. "The presents?" I ask. "You want your presents?"

She scowls, again shaking her head.

"The nurse? What?"

I take some paper and a pen from my purse. "Can you write?" I ask and she sighs, and motions me to bring the paper to her.

I pull the wheeled tray over her bed and place the paper on it, but she can't grasp the pen, she tries to hold it in her fist, like a child, but she's too weak to even make a scrawl.

She scowls again and throws the pen on the floor. She looks up at me, staring into my face as if she were trying to send me a thought. "I can read your mind," she always used to say when I was little and just about ready to do something forbidden, catching me just in time to stop me, and of course I believed her. No matter where I was, even if she was miles away, I would always cover my head with my hands when I was having a bad thought—when I was thinking about doing something I shouldn't, I would slap my hands over my ears, trying to keep the thoughts from floating through the air and straight to Virginia. I still do it occasionally. Every once in a while when I think something really horrible I'll clasp my head in my hands and shake it, trying to send the thought back down into whatever murky place it crawled up from.

She tries to speak, but makes only dry, retching sounds, and I begin to cry in my impotence.

The tears seem to infuriate her and she begins to shake her head again. Apparently I'm not supposed to cry so I smile and that infuriates her even more. She begins to wave her hands madly, and then suddenly, as if in a fit of exasperation, she reaches up and pulls the blue tube from her neck. A siren goes off on the machine, a loud, high-pitched wailing like an air-raid siren. Virginia smiles at me, an insane smile of triumph spreading over her red face and I grab the call button and begin punching it madly. I toss it back on the bed and run out into the hall looking for a nurse, but the halls are empty.

She's trying to kill herself, I think, that's why she had those restraints, and I run toward the nurses' station, looking into all the rooms, hating all the nurses—where *are* they, can't they hear that siren? It's enough to wake the dead, oh my God, what if she dies, what if she dies while Poppy's downstairs drinking coffee, what if he comes back and finds her lying there, dead, the tube wrenched from her throat, he'll think *I* did it, oh my God, don't die, don't die, I think, and finally a nurse appears, walking—*walking!*—toward Virginia's room and I run back.

"Now, now," the nurse is telling Virginia, shaking a pudgy finger at her, "we mustn't do that. You don't want your husband to see you tied up again, do you?"

The nurse turns to me. "If looks could kill . . ." she says, smiling happily, and I hear Poppy's voice in the hall, telling someone Merry Christmas, and I collapse in the chair.

22

I LOVE HAVING THE HOUSE TO MYSELF, I ALWAYS HAVE. WHEN I was little I would plan my illnesses around Virginia's bridge games or her volunteer work, coming down with a tummy ache or a fake flu on the mornings I knew she would be going out. I never overdid it; if I was too sick she wouldn't go, and if I did it too often she'd catch on.

As soon as she'd leave, I'd jump out of bed and wander from room to room, luxuriating in my freedom, searching for the perfect spot in which to make myself comfortable and then dream the day away. I'd find it—sometimes the living room couch, sometimes Poppy's armchair in the den, sometimes the velvet stool in front of Virginia's huge old mahogany vanity—and then fly away, head out to California in a covered wagon or down south to help runaway slaves or across the ocean to join Florence Nightingale in the Crimea.

Wherever I went or whatever I did, it was sure to be something huge and adventurous—I was certain there was something courageous and bold in me, something that would lead me to do great things in my life, but it was only when I was alone that I could feel it, not only feel it but *know* it, know that I was destined to do something grand with my life.

It's amazing to me how long I held on to that, how long I believed that I would eventually do something extraordinary. It always seemed just around the corner, at any moment destiny would pluck me out of the crowd, give me the opportunity to show what I was made of, how brave and good and strong I was, how uncompromisingly I believed in justice and equity, how unflinchingly I tackled prejudice and hatred, how bravely I endured hardships and deprivations to fight for my convictions.

The first glimmering of the truth came to me when I read "The Beast in the Jungle," when I realized that I might very well be just like Marcher, waiting forever for my chance to do something grand while ignoring all my opportunities to do something small but good. I began to wonder if everyone had this whatever-it-is, this sense of being special, being chosen even, of being here on earth for a specific purpose and that purpose was to do something wonderful. "Grandiosity," Greta would say, and I would slink out of her office like a worm, walking down Central Park West, toward the library, looking into all the faces I passed, wondering what was behind that blank intensity—did they too feel, *know,* that they were destined for something more, something out of the ordinary?

I suppose this is what middle age is all about, coming to the realization that one is not, after all, destined for greatness or even for anything remotely out of the ordinary, that, in fact, one might not do anything with one's life, that one might discover that one is made of nothing but fluff—illusions, dreams, hopes, desires, but nothing substantial, nothing that counts.

The doorbell rings. I look out the window and see Marion Pittsfield standing on the porch holding a large round object wrapped in tin foil. I push down the petty resentment I feel at having my solitude disturbed and go to the door.

"I saw your car," she says apologetically, "so I thought I'd bring this over."

She's been crying. Her eyes are all puffy and red behind her bifocals and she sniffles as I take the heavy package and lead her into the kitchen.

"Plum pudding," she says, "because it's Christmas."

I thank her for being so thoughtful. She wriggles out of her bulky down coat and hangs it over the back of one of the chairs and asks me if I'm okay.

"Yeah, I'm okay," I tell her. I pour out coffee for the two of us while she tells me she was at the hospital. She ran into Poppy and Cease there.

"What do you think?" she asks, tentatively. Her eyes are filled with fear and I realize she knows Virginia is dying but she won't say it unless I know, too. She's here to give me comfort, and if believing that Virginia will be all right is what I need, she'll give me that.

I offer her milk and sugar and she shakes her head.

"Black," she says. "Your mother and I always drink our coffee straight."

I clear a space for myself at the table and sit down. Mrs. Pittsfield stares at me, trying to figure out what I need, and I am afraid I will break down. It's her kindness, her palpable desire to help even when there is no help possible, that I find unbearably touching. It's so homey and sweet and it reminds me of something, something I've worked very hard to forget, something I miss terribly but refuse to recognize.

"God," she says, "it's eerie how much you look like her."

Please don't, I want to say, but instead I just nod and she grabs my hand across the table and begins to weep. Big fat tears roll down her sagging cheeks, and I'm afraid my heart will burst, will explode right through my chest and shatter all over the kitchen floor.

"I don't know what I'll do if she dies," she says. "There will be a hole in my life, a hole in the neighborhood. What will we do without her?"

She releases my hand and fumbles in her coat pocket for her cigarettes, asking me, through her sniffles, if I mind.

"No," I say as she gets up and goes straight to the cupboard where Virginia keeps her ashtrays, hundreds of them, from all over the world, little gifts from Poppy. I am surprised at how well Marion knows our kitchen, our house. Virginia always made it sound as if she didn't have any friends, didn't have any guests. Every Saturday she'd call to tell me how bleak her life was; she made it sound as if she spent all her time sitting alone in the house, waiting for the mail, waiting for Poppy to come home, waiting for Cease and me to come visit, waiting for someone to come and give her a little life. Preferably me.

Marion sits back down and lights her cigarette, tilting her head back and blowing the smoke at the ceiling, waving her hand through it as if that would make it go away.

"It's okay," I say and she sighs.

"Your mother and I were the only smokers left," she says. "At Bridge Club we had to go out on everybody's porch, even our own." She smiles. "But it wasn't so bad. We'd huddle there and giggle, like a couple of schoolgirls. It was really kind of fun, when you get down to it, like doing something we weren't supposed to do. And let's face it, when you reach our age, there isn't a whole heck of a lot you can do to get the thrill of the forbidden."

She tries to smile but begins to cry instead. I pull a tissue from the box beside the clean-air machine and hand it to her.

"We were going to take a trip this summer," she sobs. "We were going to go antiquing in Pennsylvania. It would have been the first trip she had taken without your father and she was really looking forward to it, and so was I. We were going to meet Annette and Dorothy in Atlantic City, we were going to have such a wild time, but I don't think she's going to make it, Ginger, I don't think . . ."

She stops. She blows her nose and tells me she's sorry, she's supposed to be comforting me and here she is blubbering like a big baby, but she can't help it.

"She's my best friend," she wails, covering her face with her hands. "I love her so much."

I can't stand it. I can't stand watching this woman fall apart, I can't stand watching her cry when I'm not able to, when all the tears are stuck, dammed up, threatening to overwhelm me. I am suddenly struck with the compulsion to start cleaning the house, to get down on my hands and knees and scrub the floor, to wash the windows, to clean off the guck on the stove. Suddenly, the idea of even one dirty dish, even one dustball, is anathema to me and I just want Mrs. Pittsfield to leave, to go home to her family, to let me clean.

Without saying a word, she seems to sense my need to be alone, and she uncovers her face and apologizes again, saying she'd better get home, the whole crew is there and Maggie probably forgot to check the roast, it's probably burnt to a crisp, but then again it wouldn't be Christmas without a burnt roast, it happens every year for one reason or another and every year she swears she'll switch to ham but she never does.

I help her on with her coat as she blathers on, trying to sound "normal." I nod and thank her again for the pudding. At the door she grabs me, wraps me up in her soft warm bulk, resting her head against my shoulder.

"I don't know if you know how much your mother loves you," she says.

No, I think, I don't, but I say nothing.

"She adores you," Mrs. Pittsfield says. "She absolutely adores you. I just thought I'd tell you, in case she hasn't said so herself recently," and she untangles herself, places a wet kiss on my cheek, and heads out into the snow.

23

THE KITCHEN IS SPOTLESS NOW, AND EVEN BEFORE POPPY and Cease come home, I resent them, I resent Cease's snowy boots and Poppy's stinky black rubbers messing up the shining floor. I go to the downstairs closet and pull out the vacuum cleaner, my favorite appliance, and lug it upstairs, angrily pushing aside the boxes Virginia hauled down from the attic, the boxes containing India's life.

I sweep past Virginia's room and glance in. Before her breakdown I would spend hours and hours playing in there, when it was still "their" room, when the left-hand drawers of Virginia's vanity were filled with Poppy's things: his socks, his cufflinks, his belts, the mysterious trinkets from the war, little medals and foreign coins. On Virginia's side there were boxes and boxes of what she called "junk jewelry" but to me they were treasures; going into their room was like entering Ali Baba's cave, a marvelous world of beauty and magic.

I haven't been in her room in decades. I never cleaned it; once she closed her door to us I never felt any curiosity about what was going on in there. I felt only dread, knowing that if I opened her door I would see something I didn't want to see, feel something I didn't want to feel, and I would quickly pass by, the odor of stale cigarette smoke and mildew assaulting me, seeping out from under the door, a musty, attic-like smell, the smell of things forgotten, things abandoned, and I would hurry past before it could grab me, racing into the bathroom and scrubbing the sky-blue tiles viciously, hysterically.

I stick my head through the doorway and look around. The end table next to the bed is littered with glasses and dirty ashtrays, the dark wood marred with white rings and long black burns. It's a miracle she hasn't burned the house down.

I take a deep breath and enter the room, sneakily, like a spy or a thief. It's idiotic, but I feel like someone in a horror movie, someone entering the room where we know the monster lurks, and I want to shout at myself, "Don't go in there, you fool!" even though it's insane, even though this is just the room where a lonely, defeated woman hid from the world.

The room is a mess. Clothes tossed in a heap on the chaise in the alcove; shoes and stockings lying about on the floor; dust everywhere. On the wall over the dresser she has her "rogues' gallery," photographs of us all: Poppy in his Air Force uniform, India in a brocade caftan, Cease on the beach in a sailor outfit, little Roger in his bassinet. A young, beautiful Virginia smiles confidently in what must have been either her graduation or engagement photograph. In the corner of the frame, she has tucked a photo of me and I realize Marion

Pittsfield was right, it *is* eerie how alike we look. I stare at the two photos, wondering how it can be that we look so much alike and yet Virginia is beautiful and I am not. How is that possible? Our features are almost exactly the same, but there is something missing in me, a light, a joy, a warmth, I don't know. It's almost as if there's a lifelessness in my photo—that girl doesn't seem real to me, she seems guarded, hidden, refusing to reveal what, if anything, is inside her.

I walk over to the vanity and sit down on the stool. Her makeup and perfume bottles are arranged neatly but are covered with a thick layer of grime. She obviously hasn't touched them in years—why bother, she must think, who ever looks at me?

I feel like an interloper. Even though Virginia's room has never been forbidden to me, it was off-limits, not because she didn't want to let me in but rather because I wanted to stay out. I guiltily open the top drawer of the vanity. The boxes are still there, piled haphazardly, white boxes, gold boxes, blue boxes with the gold-lettered name of some defunct Detroit jeweler. I take them all out and spread them on Virginia's unmade bed. I remember a little towheaded girl, standing by the side of the bed, watching Virginia look at herself in the mirror, tilting her head as she clipped on first one ruby-red rhinestone earring and then another. She would look at me in the mirror and wink, beckoning me to come to her and she would open the drawer and take out the greatest treasure of all, the tiara. "Queen for a Day!" she'd declare, placing it on my head and kissing my forehead and I would dance around the room, thinking I was indeed a princess, a plain little princess who would surprise everyone and grow up to be a beautiful queen, just like my mother. Virginia would laugh and get up and dance with me, twirling me around and around, tossing me up in the air and then hugging me close to her chest, laughing and tickling my head with kisses, calling me her "little dumpling." "Scrumptious!" she'd say and pretend to gobble me up.

Who will remember that Virginia? I've spent most of my life trying to forget her, because to remember her seemed almost masochistic, to remember her was to long for her and to long for her was to long for something that was dead.

I look into the mirror, wanting to see that little towheaded girl bedecked with jewels, with bright red circles of rouge on my cheeks and Virginia's rhinestone tiara teetering on my head, but instead I see myself, as I am, a rather plain-looking woman, neither old nor young. I can see neither the past nor the future, what I was or who I will be. "Tell me what to *do*," I implore the woman in the mirror, but of course she is just as confused as I, the mirror is not a magical one, it only tells me what I already know.

I open the other drawers. More boxes, bottles of caked nail polish, torn gloves, belts rolled up in coils, little mending packets from European hotels, little slivers of glass filled with perfume. A photo of her father, in a tarnished silver frame, standing in front of The Willows. I pick up a package of matches from the Ritz, in Paris, and I wonder if that's where her Italian lover stayed and I shudder, tossing the matches back with disgust.

If I were in anyone's room but Virginia's I would be ecstatic. Here it all is, her history, her clothes, her photographs, her keepsakes, her joys, her triumphs and even her humiliations, all here, all the little pieces of her life but I don't want to put them together. Who is she? Is she the drunken, self-pitying, whining woman full of need who calls me once a week to beat me with her misery? If so, who is that woman Marion Pittsfield was talking about? Who is the woman Poppy so adores?

I open the top drawer on the other side of the vanity, what

used to be Poppy's side. This is new for me, I don't know what to expect, what Virginia has hidden away in the drawers where Poppy's socks used to be. In a way, I feel obligated to look, as if it were my duty. The detective in me, the searcher, is excited, but the daughter in me is filled with dread. The detective rubs her hands and says, "Information!" while the daughter holds her hands over her head and says, "Pain!"

In the top drawer, I am surprised to find a bit of my own history, elementary school report cards, Valentines made from faded red construction paper and yellowed doilies, the note I wrote her when I was seven years old and running away from home forever because I broke the heel off her best pair of shoes while playing dress-up.

The second drawer is filled with Cease's childhood things: Mother's Day poems and Boy Scout crafts—a carved wooden ashtray, a beaded belt, a soap dish made from broken tiles—all our little love offerings, kept handy, and I wonder how often she looks at them, how often she takes them out and holds on to them as she slides down into the murk of self-pity.

In the bottom drawer she has tucked away a few gaily wrapped boxes, Christmas presents she never gave. "Emergency gifts," she used to call them, in case someone unexpected showed up with a gift for her—the babysitter, an out-of-town friend, a client of Poppy's. I feel the childish urge to unwrap them, to peek, to see if there's anything for me, but I know there isn't. I can tell just by looking at the boxes what they are: the flat one is a bridge set, the fat square one is a Christmas ornament, the long narrow one is filled with scented soaps. There is nothing for me in any of them but I want to steal them, to take them back to New York and gloat over them.

I slam the drawer shut and turn around to look again at her photo. If Virginia were a stranger to me, more of a stranger than she actually is, what would I make of all this? How would I turn this room into a person, how could anyone looking at all this junk see the woman she once was?

"You should write a book about *me*," her voice says and although I know she's not here, I look at the doorway, expecting to see her standing there, drink in one hand and cigarette in the other, dressed in her polka-dot hospital gown.

"I can't," I tell the voice, and it says, "Why not? If you're so interested in women who can't do, what's wrong with me? I certainly haven't done anything."

"Virginia, I've told you a million times, I only write about dead people," I say and she laughs.

"You can't use that excuse anymore," the voice tells me. "I'm dead."

In my mind, I see her lying in the hospital bed, smiling triumphantly as she yanks the tube out of her neck. She can't be dead, she can't. If she dies now I will see that vision for the rest of my life, it will wake me up at night and follow me around all day, every time I close my eyes I will see her grinning and waving that tube at me. "I did it," her eyes will say, "I finally *did* something."

It's the room. It's haunted. One doesn't need to be dead to be a ghost; hasn't Virginia's spirit trailed me about from city to city, following me everywhere, watching everything I do and egging on the Panel of Judges, waking them up if they've drifted off to sleep long enough for me to attempt to enjoy myself? There was a time when I even wished she *would* die, when I thought I would be free, that I could live if she would die. It was as if I thought I owed my life to her, that I must live my life *for* her, and I refused, refused to do anything that might give her pleasure, that she could claim for herself, that she could grab and carry up here to hide away with Poppy's plaques and Cease's toys. I was like a selfish child, screaming, "It's *mine!*" refusing to share even the tiniest part of it with

Virginia, making all my choices based not on what I wanted but rather on what I thought Virginia wouldn't want. But even that didn't work. Virginia's voracity knew no bounds, made no sense, I couldn't trick her into not wanting my life, because it had nothing to do with desire, it had to do with hunger, and no matter how bland I made my life, how boring and dry and tasteless, she gobbled it up.

How I loathed us both. I hated myself for being ungenerous, for holding on to my pallid little life as if it were something of great value, for refusing to share any of it with her. "You are so selfish," she would say when her spirit appeared in my apartment, perched on the wardrobe door, swinging back and forth while I dressed to go out dancing, to go to the theater, to hear some music. "You had your chance!" I would shout and she would hang her head, looking sad and forlorn, and I would feel vile and horrible. What did she want, after all? Just to be let into my life, just for me to share it with her; but I couldn't do it, I thought sharing was impossible with Virginia, I was terrified she would take whatever I gave her and never give it back, and so I made sure that there was nothing in my life I would mind losing.

I didn't want it to be like that. All my life I had longed for a mother I could trust, a mother I could run to with my little problems, a mother who would tell me what to do, tell me what life was all about, advise me, guide me, help me. It never occurred to me that Virginia didn't know, that she was as baffled by life as I was, just as untutored as I. I thought she was holding something back, greedily hiding away the secrets of life she should be sharing with me. What did I know—I thought all mothers were like the one in *Little Women,* wise and kind and ceaselessly giving, that was what a mother was supposed to be like and, to my great shame, I resented the hell out of Virginia for not being Mrs. March. If only Virginia could be like Marmee, I told myself, I could share my life with her, for Marmee would never take her daughters' lives and hide them under her bed.

It seems insane now, but it was real enough to me at the time, as if Virginia and I were locked in some sort of battle to the death, fighting over my life as if it were a thing, a dress we both wanted, a piece of jewelry, a piece of property. I had no sympathy for either of us, I was locked in the battle and the only time I was free was when I was immersed in someone else's life, when I was, ironically, doing to some hapless dead woman precisely what I feared Virginia was trying to do to me, when I enveloped myself in someone else's life so I wouldn't have to think about my own.

I wish I hadn't been so frightened of her. All she wanted was life, she wanted to feel alive, and no matter how much I gave her or how much she stole, from me or anyone else, it would never be enough. It would never be enough because it wasn't hers.

And now she's dying. If I could stuff my life in a box and wrap it up in Christmas paper and take it to her, I would, but it's too late. Poppy thinks she'll live but I know better, I know she'll never come home again.

Love. How is it that something so beautiful could turn so ugly? How is it that something we both wanted so much could have been so impossible to have? I climb into her bed and curl up in the center, pulling the reeking sheets up to my chin, and weep.

24

REVEREND ATWELL IS SPEAKING ABOUT VIRGINIA AS IF HE knew her; he is talking about the Virginia of thirty years ago, the altar lady at St. Thomas's, the woman who made potholders for the annual church bazaar. He touches upon her weaknesses, never mentioning them by name, simply acknowledging that she, like all of us, had them.

The service is being held in the cemetery chapel rather than in St. Thomas's, and I'm not sure why, but I remember there's a reason, Poppy told me but I haven't heard much of anything anyone has said over the past few days. The chapel is new and austere and institutional, it looks and feels more like a gymnasium than a place of worship, and I can't rid myself of the feeling that as soon as they wheel Virginia's coffin out, the decoration committee will come in to hang crepe-paper streamers for a pep rally.

Poppy and Cease and I are sitting in the front row, at a right angle to the open coffin: oak, with a rose satin interior. Virginia is lying there, dressed in her white and blue Chanel suit, her favorite when she still cared about things like that. "You pick something out," Poppy told me and I dutifully went upstairs and looked through her closet, trying to find something that didn't need dry cleaning, something that didn't have cigarette burns, something that wasn't balled-up like a rag, but it was impossible, there wasn't a garment in that huge closet that wasn't soiled, or stained, or burned or filthy. The Chanel suit, at least, had the burns in the back, where no one would see them, and all I can think about, as I look at her lying in that coffin, bloated and white, is that she's meeting her Maker with a burn-hole on her butt.

The altar lady of whom Reverend Atwell is speaking, that potholder-making den mother, would be mortified. Like most mothers, she was of the clean-underwear-in-case-of-accident school, and she would have been horrified if anyone had suggested that someday she would lie in a coffin in a suit not only full of burn holes but cut away in the back as well, so the mortician could fit it to her puffy, fat corpse, the crowning degradation to her unspeakably degrading last days—tied up, helpless, unable to move or speak or eat or breathe or even pee, her weary eyes begging for relief, begging, I thought, to be set free but Poppy wouldn't hear of it. "They want me to let them pull the plug," he wept. "That would be like killing her!" and so she lingered on and on and on, huge tears seeping out of the corners of her eyes, dripping down her face and into her ears, and I would wipe them away while Cease sobbed out his confession, over and over again and Poppy stood by the side of the bed, clutching her hand, completely oblivious to Cease and me, not even batting an eye as Cease went on and on about Roger. Poppy just stared at her, visibly wasting away himself, and I feared I would lose them both, but finally even Poppy could take it no more, when she began to be racked by horrible, soundless coughs, her whole body shuddering in the bed as if she were being jolted by electric shocks, her face turning red and then purple, her eyes disappearing up into her brow, the white balls lined with long slashes of red, it was unendurable, and the next time Dr. Keller suggested a morphine drip, Poppy held his head in his hands, weeping, and nodded.

He didn't want to let her go. He wanted to hold on to her forever, and I feared he would try to go with her. At the hospital, the night she died, he wouldn't even let Cease and me in her room, he closed the door, shut us out, as if to punish us for not loving her enough. We stood outside, looking in through the glass window. Reverend Atwell was there, no doubt muttering something soothing, and Virginia lay there, with a pained expression on her face while Poppy sat in a chair next to the bed, leaning over with his head on her chest. At one point, she looked over at us and we smiled and waved, like a pair of idiots, but what else could we do? Finally, Reverend Atwell motioned us in and we slipped in like naughty children and approached her bed. "Oh, Ginny," Poppy was crying, "please don't go, please don't go," and she began to shudder, her body racked by those soundless coughs, and she closed her eyes and died.

Poppy couldn't believe it. He couldn't believe she could possibly leave him. It had never occurred to him that she might go before him; after all, he was seven years older than she, and women invariably outlived men. This had not been part of his plan; he had thought about death, of course, but the death he thought about was his own, not hers, she was supposed to be there, with him, at the end, she was supposed to weep over his grave, not he over hers.

Reverend Atwell is saying something about the gentleness of death and Cease lets out a snort and I think about Cassie's story of her grandmother's death, how she was at home, lying in her bed with her nurse sitting in a chair by the window, reading aloud to her from some thriller. Suddenly, Cassie's grandmother began laughing and smiling and waving, and the nurse called in Cassie and her mother and they all stood around the bed, watching as her grandmother happily greeted, one by one, her dead husband, her son who died in the war, her sister, her face growing more and more animated as she recognized first one and then another of her loved ones. "This is the God's honest truth," Cassie said. "It was as if the wrinkles disappeared from her face, she was positively glowing, and then suddenly she laughed and stopped breathing. It was so incredibly beautiful, so moving, that none of us could cry, we just felt this overwhelming happiness for her." "Just like *Buddenbrooks*," I said, running to my bookcase and pulling down my copy, searching for the passage in which Mann describes the elderly Frau Consul's death in almost the exact same way. I found it, and read it to Cassie, and we both sat there, amazed and stunned and covered with goose bumps. "It's almost enough to make you believe," Cassie said, and I look at Virginia's face, her mouth set in a disapproving scowl, her puffy cheeks painted with rouge, and I begin to weep, not because she's dead but because even in death she couldn't get a break, she couldn't joyfully sail over the edge into the waiting arms of her beloved father and little Roger, she had to go choking and gasping and racked with pain.

I look around the room. Melanie is here, with Frank. She's right, he's "as cute as ever," his round, high-cheeked cherub's face glowing and youthful, showing no signs whatsoever of the hell he apparently endured. They're sitting near the back, holding hands, and I am gripped with a nauseating wave of envy, not the intense, longing envy of desire but rather the dispiriting envy of lack.

Reverend Atwell is finished; he is introducing Poppy, who

insisted on giving a speech, although I don't know how he'll make it through it without collapsing, without falling apart. He can barely say her name without dissolving into hiccupy sobs. He worked on the speech all last night, I could hear him in his office, pecking away slowly, letter by letter, and I remembered Virginia sitting at the kitchen table, waving her drink toward his office, saying, "He'll die before he gets to me." I lay there in bed, staring out the window at the darkness, and I hoped that her spirit hadn't fled too fast, that it had lingered long enough to see Poppy, hard at work, finally getting to her.

Poppy stands up and Cease gets up and helps him to the podium. I feel a little lump of tenderness bob about inside of me—an outsider could never see the change in Cease, but to me it's obvious a softening is taking place, a bond is forming between Poppy and Cease, and I get a burning, tight constriction in my throat as I watch Cease tenderly escort Poppy up to the lectern.

I am amazed by how many people are here. The seats are all filled, it's standing room only, and I wonder who these people are. They can't all be nut cases, floating from funeral to funeral. "Everybody loved your mother," Marion Pittsfield said at the funeral home, and apparently she was right. The room is filled with her friends, with women I didn't know existed. "I didn't think she *had* any friends," I said to Marion, and she tilted her head and said, "What nonsense! Who told you that?" "Virginia," I said and she laughed and rolled her eyes and said, "Oh, well. You know how she was when she got in one of her moods," and I wanted crawl into the basement of the mortuary, climb into a coffin, and die of shame. To Marion and her other friends, Virginia's despair was just a "mood," but to me it was her whole life.

I always thought she was so desperate for me to *see* her but now I realize she didn't want me to see all of her, she only wanted me to see the part she wouldn't show to anyone else, the ugly, bitter, grasping part of herself that no one could possibly love. And I'll never know why. I suppose Greta would tell me it had something to do with wanting the unconditional love from me that she never got from her mother, or some such thing, and I guess I would buy that, but I think there was something else, something more. It's crazy, I suppose, but now that she's dead, I think she was trying to *honor* me with her pain, that she somehow trusted that eventually I would understand and forgive her. But I was too frightened by it, too stupid to see what she was doing.

I look at her, lying on a bed of rose satin. Why couldn't she just *tell* me what she needed, why did she have to try to bury us both in her wretchedness?

I wonder if this was my test, if being large enough to help Virginia carry her burden was my test in life. If so, I failed, and I wish I could get up and shake her, shake her until she woke up, opened her eyes, and said, "What's going on here?"

Poppy clears his throat. "I want to thank you all for coming," he says. He turns his head toward the coffin and I close my eyes. "Don't look!" I think, but he has, and his voice becomes thick and phlegmy, filled with tears. I open my eyes, reluctantly, I don't want to see him hunched over the podium, weeping, snot dripping from his nose, I don't want to see this and neither does anyone else, the pain and discomfort in the room, the nervous embarrassment is palpable, even Reverend Atwell is blushing and staring at the shiny black tips of his shoes peeking out from under his vestments.

"You didn't know her!" Poppy cries. "Nobody *knew* her, nobody even tried to know her. She wasn't what she seemed, she wasn't what she appeared to be on the outside, that woman with all the 'weaknesses,' she was more than that." He's got his voice back now, his lawyer voice. We are no longer mourners but a jury, a jury he must convince of Virginia's innocence, a jury that must acquit her before she goes before the final Judge.

"She was special," he says. "She was kind and gentle and loving but she was fragile, she was like a beautiful crystal figurine, lovely and elegant but utterly breakable. She belonged in a different world, this world was too harsh for her, too brutal, and I'm not excusing her for not being strong enough to bear up under it. I used to tell her, 'Ginny, we live in the world we live in and have to make the best of it.' And she tried, she tried to be a good wife and a good mother and a good neighbor, she tried to be like everybody else, to fit in, but she took life so hard it was impossible. I used to make fun of her, to try to make her see it wasn't so important, that her disappointments needn't take on catastrophic significance, but I only hurt her more. 'Life is too serious to take it seriously,' I'd say and she'd laugh, she'd be a good sport about it, but she'd cry herself to sleep at night, until, finally, she didn't have any tears left. And so she seemed to become hard, hard and withdrawn and unloving, but she was just the opposite."

He pauses and looks around the room, resting his gaze on Cease and me, and Cease begins to shudder, as if he feared Poppy was going to point at him and announce to the world, or at least the gathered crowd, that he, Cease, was the true culprit, the murderer not only of little Roger but of Virginia as well, that Poppy would, like Perry Mason, pull from his pocket the Lego piece, and wave it in front of the mourners in triumph.

Instead, he moves his gaze to Virginia's body. "We don't know what to do when we come across a soul that gentle, that vulnerable," he says. "We try to toughen it up, for its own good, we try to make it fit our world. We just can't let it be, and when we break it again and again, when we've broken it beyond repair, we throw up our hands in disgust and turn away."

Everyone in the room is weeping now. Poppy has done his job, he's made us all feel personally responsible for Virginia's demise, not least of all himself. The room reeks of guilt and shame and he sniffles loudly and looks around the room.

"She was a good woman," he says. "I just wanted you all to know that. We're having a kind of buffet thing over at our house after the burial, and you're all invited. She would have wanted that," and he shuffles slowly back to his seat. Someone, somewhere unseen, turns on taped organ music and Reverend Atwell returns to the podium to organize the crowd for the burial, and I slip out, nodding to the muttered condolences I hear as I pass, to prepare the "buffet thing."

25

THERE ISN'T MUCH TO DO. THE KITCHEN IS OVERFLOWING with food, casseroles and cold meat platters and ten different kinds of homemade bread from the women who got bread machines for Christmas this year.

I was happy to come home and do this; I didn't want to watch as the coffin lid was closed. I didn't want to see Virginia lowered into the ground, and I especially didn't want to see the neat mound of dirt next to her grave, ready to be shoveled over her. I didn't want to hear the thudding of the earth on her coffin. There's something so final about the dirt—it's as if it will smother not only her body but her spirit as well and I like to think that her spirit, at least, lives on, free from that bitter prison in which it was trapped for so long.

I look around the kitchen, half expecting to see Virginia's shadow hovering around the bottles of booze I've placed neatly on a silver tray, but of course there's nothing there. The house has never seemed so quiet, and I imagine I can hear my own blood chugging through my veins, slowly and rhythmically, like a freighter's engine out on the lake, thumpa, thumpa, thumpa, reminding me that I am alive and she is dead.

I think about calling Michael, giving him the opportunity to come through for me, but I'm terrified he won't. Terrified that, on top of everything else I'm going through now I would be forced to face the truth that our whatever-it-is, our "us," is nothing but a fantasy, and, frankly, it's a fantasy I'd like to hold on to for just a little while longer, just long enough to get me through this and back home, back to New York, back to myself.

Besides, he should call me. He should have sensed that there was something wrong, that I'm in need. If he really loved me, he would have known it without my having to tell him, or so I tell myself, even though I know it's absurd, that kind of telepathic communication is a nice touch in movies and romance novels but I have yet to see it work in real life, at least not in *my* real life. Even though I know it's ridiculous, that even if it were possible to send him a message, there isn't enough "brain space" available for it to get through—his mind is so cluttered with thoughts of himself and his fame and his "bits" that all I'd get is a busy signal, but even so, I keep hoping. I close my eyes and clutch my fists into tight balls and strain with all my might, sending my need hurtling through space, where I hope it will hit a satellite and bounce back to earth, back to New York, where Michael is calmly walking down a street, pausing at every third bus stop to admire himself in his pocket T, only to be suddenly gripped by an overwhelming terror in the pit of his stomach. He'll bend over double, leaning on the bus stop, thinking, "Oh, my God, Ginger's in trouble, she *needs* me!" and hobble to the closest phone to call me.

I feel somewhat ashamed for setting up this silly and impossible quest for Michael to prove his devotion, and also for even thinking about using Virginia's death as an excuse to get my needs met.

Despite all my talk about wanting to feel again, I'm trying very hard not to right now. I'm not trying to avoid the pain; that, in fact, I would almost welcome—grief, after all, is acceptable after the death of a loved one. If I could let myself go to the grief, no one, not even the Panel of Judges, could fault me, unless of course I went too far, got a little operatic about it, tearing my hair and rending my garments and shrieking through the night. No, what I am trying desperately to avoid, to stifle, is that snotty little girl inside me, that wicked little brat locked up down in the darkest cellar of my soul, where she's gleefully cavorting about in the gloom, dancing and singing at the top of her lungs. "Ding-dong, the witch is dead," she sings and I think I should run down to the beach and out onto the ice, far, far out until I can't even see the shore, until the ice cracks and I fall through. For the truth is, how can I drown out that voice without drowning myself? I can't. She's as much a part of me as any other part, a part I hate and who in turn hates me, hates me for stifling her, trying to kill her off, for never giving her a chance to live. But how could I? She was too unruly, too uncontrollable.

Everybody hated her, especially Virginia, and I wanted Virginia's love more than anything in the world, and I would have killed not only that girl but half a dozen others if it would have helped. It didn't, of course, the only thing I succeeded in doing was creating a very angry little child-monster, a monster nobody could possibly love.

"Shut up," I tell her, pulling out the ice bucket and scrubbing the layer of film at the bottom, and she goes away, but she'll be back. She's been haunting me ever since Virginia died, popping up at the most inopportune moments, ruthlessly laughing aloud when someone comes sniffling over with another tin of meatloaf, and I have to flee upstairs and hide. Fortunately, she didn't make an appearance at the funeral, and I suppose for that I should be grateful.

Everything is ready. The house sparkles, it's a house that would make the women on *Lady of Charm* glow with pride. Even Virginia's room is clean. Poppy has invited Virginia's friends to come and take her clothes, her costume jewelry, her purses and hats. I tried to talk him out of it, telling him her clothes were a little the worse for wear, but he wants to give it all away.

I fill the bucket with ice and place it on the tray with the booze. "That's what she would have wanted," Poppy said, "she always liked a lively party," and I can almost see her, standing next to the counter in her stained bathrobe, waving her drink in the air and saying, "Always plenty of screwdrivers at Chez Moore!"

A car pulls up in the driveway, and then another. The doorbell rings and I begin to laugh—"Ding-dong, the witch is dead," I think and throw my hands over my head, trying to push the bad thoughts down, but what if I can't? What if I start laughing? What if I go to the door to meet these bereaved friends of Virginia's and Poppy's and I'm laughing hysterically, meeting their condolences with loud cackles of glee? And what about Poppy? If he saw me laughing he'd have a fit, he'd hate me forever, I never could explain to him that this isn't how I feel, not entirely, yes, there's a part of me that's glad but it's only a tiny part, the rest of me is bereft, the rest of me wants Virginia here more than anything else in the world, because *she's* the only one who would understand this.

The doorbell rings again and I grab Virginia's mink from the closet and run out the back door, fast, down to the beach.

26

IT'S BEEN A MILD WINTER. THERE'S A LITTLE RIDGE OF ICE along the shore of the lake, but nothing substantial, nothing I can hide in.

The boat hoists have been pulled out of the water and stand like some kind of steel Stonehenge on the south end of the beach. I have always wondered how they got them out of the water, but for some reason I never asked anyone. It was the kind of question that seemed intriguing at the time but never held my interest long enough to ask it.

I climb up on one of the hoists and sit on the wooden plank, facing south, toward the bridge. The way home.

A sickle moon is rising over Canada, a little sliver of white in the still-blue sky and I wonder what comes next, what comes after death. Is there anything beyond this?

I wonder if there is an afterlife, if Virginia and India are up in heaven right now, having a little chat, if India is telling her the truth and Virginia is forgiving her, what difference does it make now that they're both dead? I wonder if Virginia's life would have been any different if she had known, would she have been a different person if she hadn't been weighted down with the burden of India's supposed heroism, if she could have just felt the rage of her abandonment instead of having to sacrifice it to a Greater Cause?

I'll never know. "What if" doesn't count for the dead; if their souls live on, they know everything, and if they don't live on, if you're just dead, then it doesn't make any difference at all to them, it only makes a difference to us, the ones left behind, the ones who wish we could have been better, could have been more loving, more generous, more kind.

"What makes a life notable?" This is the question I ask my students at the beginning of the term and they give me the usual answers: accomplishment, fame, infamy, courage, eccentricity, power, glory, leadership. I assign them Anne Frank's diary and they all grumble and groan—what is this kid stuff?—they read that in junior high, for God's sake, they want to work on their projects, they don't want to be bothered with this pedantic philosophical bullshit. Some of them never see the point, they think I want them to give me a book report, to tell me what it's "about," but that isn't what I want at all; in fact, I don't "want" anything, unless it is for them to see that for the biographer, and for the autobiographer, there is only one thing that makes a life notable, and that is truth. Not necessarily Truth with a capital T, for that is fluctuating, amorphous, what is True today, this second, may not be True tomorrow. Anne Frank's diary is so true, so genuine, that one cannot read it without feeling her presence, without knowing that this person was *alive*.

Among Virginia's things, I found a diary, brown leather with a little gilt clasp. Before she died I couldn't open it. I felt ashamed and weak for only being able to read about her pain when I wouldn't have to do anything about it, but I needn't have worried, when I opened the diary there was nothing there, except her name, her name and a couple hundred blank lined pages, and that silence was sadder than anything she could have written, anything I could have imagined.

I hear footsteps crunching in the snow and turn around to see Melanie mincing her way across the beach.

"I thought you'd be here," she says, climbing up on the plank and shivering. "Just like old times."

I nod. "Except Maggie Pittsfield isn't here with a box of her father's candy."

"And Goober. Remember that mangy dog?"

I nod again and think of Fritz, of the two dogs running around on the ice, slipping and sliding and scurrying back to the beach to roll around in ecstasy on the dead fish.

"You okay?" she asks and I say yes, yes, I'm okay.

"I can't believe we actually used to ice skate out there," she says, pointing to the lake. "We must have been out of our minds. We could have fallen through and disappeared until spring."

"Well, we thought we were invulnerable," I say. "And besides, our mothers told us not to."

"I guess they weren't as stupid as we thought," she says, starting to giggle. "Remember how we used to call your mother 'the wrath of God'? She was always after you to change your clothes: 'You look like the wrath of God in that outfit!'"

I laugh. "Poor Virginia," I say. "She's going up to Heaven looking like the wrath of God herself—there were cigarette burns in her suit."

Melanie's eyes shine mischievously, and with an incredibly sweet, tender, and childlike motion she covers her mouth with her hand.

"Oh, God," she says. "She'll be *mortified*."

We begin to laugh, and I realize, suddenly, how futile and wrong it has been for me to try to escape from the silly schoolgirl I once was. I have always been so ashamed of her, so ashamed that I was once stupid and giddy and boy-crazy and consumed with dreams of stardom. So terrified of her rage, her fury at being locked away, first by Virginia, who held her prisoner, who made her watch her daily descent into hell, and then by myself, by my fear of being humiliated, of being weak, of being undignified.

I suppose that's why I keep reassigning *The Diary of a Young Girl*. It has nothing to do with the time, the situation, the hell she lived in; it has to do with her incredible humanity, her wholeness, her ability to fearlessly *be* who she is.

"What are you thinking?" Melanie asks.

I shrug. "I don't know," I say. "I'm so confused. It seems I've spent my whole life trying to figure out some secret about life. Not the meaning of it, that's too grand for me, too impossible. It's more like a little secret, a secret that never seemed important to anyone but me."

"Like what?" she asks.

"Oh, I don't know how to explain it. It's this compulsion of mine, this need to find the secret of why certain women can't *do*."

"Maybe they're tired," Melanie says.

"What?"

"Maybe they're just *tired*. Maybe they're trying so hard to do the wrong thing they're too exhausted to do the right one."

Could it be that simple? Could it be that I've spent the last twenty years of my life trying to find the key to a door that wasn't even locked in the first place?

I sigh and she asks me when I'm going home.

"In a couple of weeks," I say. "I'm just going to make sure Poppy and Cease are set up and then I'll leave."

"Cease?" she asks. "He's staying?"

"Yes," I say. "He wants to stay. And Poppy wants him to."

"Well, that'll be interesting," she says and we both laugh. She puts her arm around me and we sit there, staring out at the lake.

I point at the ice. "Once," I tell Melanie, "when I was on my way to see my shrink, I saw a guy dancing on a patch of ice on Ninetieth Street. Two women were hanging out of a window on the other side of the street, laughing at him, and he was having the greatest time, dancing and singing and just plain cutting up for those women. I had this kind of flash of desire to join him . . ."

"A *stranger?*" she asks. "In *New York?*"

"Melanie, New York's not that bad. And that isn't the point. The point isn't that I wanted to dance with *him*, the point is I wanted to *dance*. What difference would it have made, I would never have seen any of those people again, I could have just run up to him, spun around, and gone my merry way. But I couldn't. I couldn't do it."

"Is there a point to this?" Melanie asks.

I nod. "It seemed like such a definitive moment," I tell her. "I felt so *old*, Melanie, not just old, but dead, in a way. I felt as if that had been my last chance. If I had taken it, I would have had many more, but because I didn't, I would get none."

She nods. "That's the way I used to feel every time I slipped," she says. "Like I screwed up my last chance. I was half-dead anyway, why not drink myself to death?"

"But," she says, jumping off the boat hoist and down onto the snow-covered sand, "here I am, living proof that there are more chances than you think."

She runs down to the shore and beckons to me. She begins dancing about on the rim of ice and I run to her, Virginia's mink flapping behind me, and we slip and slide and fall and laugh so hard we cry.

ABOUT THE AUTHOR

Rebecca Stowe is the author of *Not the End of the World*. This is her second novel.

Available in Norton Paperback Fiction